DOUBLE

DOUBLE

by Jenny Valentine

HYPERION
NEW YORK

First U.S. Edition, 2012

10 9 8 7 6 5 4 3 2 1

G475-5664-5-11349

Printed in the United States of America

Originally published in Great Britain in 2010 by HarperCollins Publishers Ltd.
under the title *The Double Life of Cassiel Roadnight*

Library of Congress Cataloging-in-Publication Data

Valentine, Jenny.

[Double life of Cassiel Roadnight]

Double / Jenny Valentine.—1st ed.

p. cm.

Summary: When sixteen-year-old Chap is mistaken for a missing boy,
he leaves the home where he has been living temporarily and takes on this new identity,
not knowing that it is as dangerous and uncertain as the life he left behind.

ISBN 978-1-4231-4714-5 (alk. paper)

[1. Impostors and imposture—Fiction. 2. Identity—Fiction.
3. Missing children—Fiction. 4. England—Fiction.] I. Title.

PZ7.V25213Do 2012

[Fic]—dc22

2011010027

Reinforced binding

Visit www.hyperionteens.com

SUSTAINABLE FORESTRY INITIATIVE

Certified Fiber
Sourcing

www.sfiprogram.org

THIS LABEL APPLIES TO TEXT STOCK

For Maikki Ranger, my accidental twin

DOUBLE

ONE

I didn't choose to be him. I didn't pick Cassiel Roadnight out of a lineup of possible people who looked just like me. I just let it happen. I just wanted it to be true. That's all I did wrong, at the beginning.

I was in a hostel, a stop-off for impossible kids in east London somewhere. I'd been there a couple of days, walked in off the streets half starved, because I had to. They were still trying to get hold of me. They were still trying to find out who I was.

I wasn't going to tell them.

It was a tired place run by tired people. It smelled of cigarettes and floor polish and soup. They gave me old clothes, washed thin and mended and almost the right size. They asked me lots of questions in return for two meals and a dry place to sleep.

I tried to be grateful, but I didn't speak to them.

They locked me in a storeroom for fighting. Hot and airless, four pale walls, a shut and rusted filing cabinet, a shelf piled with papers, a stack of chairs.

The boy I fought with was hurt. That's why I was locked up, really, for winning. You're not allowed to do that. I don't remember his name. I don't remember what the fight was about, even.

I was in the storeroom for over two hours. I wanted to wreck it. I watched myself doing it, somewhere in my head.

I heard one of them coming, saw the wavering, moss-colored shape of her through the mottled glass of the door. I banged on it hard. She stopped and turned and took a quick breath of her disappointed air.

Her voice was small and jumpy. "What do you want?" she said.

"I want you to let me out."

"I can't do that."

I put my head against the cold skin of the wall. "Please help me," I said.

"Are you hurt?" she said. "Are you bleeding?"

"I'm thirsty."

She didn't say anything.

"You can't deprive me of water."

"I'll go and ask," she said, and through the glass she warped and gathered and was gone.

I counted to four hundred and thirty-eight.

When she came back, she had someone else with her. They unlocked the door and swooped in with a plastic cup half filled with water. I drank it down in one gulp. It wasn't enough.

The man had a hook nose and loose, curly hair. I'd seen him before, but not her. He sounded like keys jangling.

He said, "Have you finished fighting?"

I shrugged. "Probably not."

I didn't like the way the woman was looking at me. I stared back so she would stop, but she didn't. Between us there was just the blood in my ears, pounding and pumping, and the look on her face.

She kept her eyes on me while she spoke to the man and as she left the room. "Hang on a minute, would you? I'll be right back."

The man sat in one of the chairs, shifting, trying hard to look relaxed. He leaned toward me and his black eyes blinked, quick and vigilant, like a bird's. I wondered if he minded being alone with me. I wondered if he was afraid.

"Why won't you tell us your name?" he said.

I pretended he wasn't there. I pretended he wasn't talking.

"I'm Gordon," he said. "And the lady's name is Ginny."

"Well done," I said. "Good for you."

"And you are?" he said.

I looked at my shoes, somebody else's shoes, black and lumpy and scuffed. I wondered how many nobodies had worn them. I felt the fabric of someone else's shirt against my skin,

5

nobody else's trousers. How was I supposed to know?

I smiled. "I'm nobody," I said.

"Oh, come on," he said. "Everyone is somebody."

It was amazing, really, how he could be so sure of that.

It was the fifth of November when I found out I wasn't who I thought I was. I remember the exact moment. I didn't know myself anymore. I asked a man for the time so I could commit it to memory. He looked at his watch and told me it was twenty-five past seven. Then he just went back to his newspaper.

I said, "Do you know me? Do you know who I am?" I knew he wouldn't, but I needed him so badly to say yes.

I could tell he wasn't concentrating on his reading anymore. He just had his eyes on the words while he waited for me to go away. He was scared.

The Ginny woman came back with something in her hand, a piece of paper. "Can I have a word?" she said.

Gordon got up and they left me in the room on my own again. I could hear them on the other side of the door. They were whispering, but I could still hear.

She said, "I only saw it this morning. Pure coincidence."

"Bloody hell."

"He's been gone nearly two years."

"Well. I. Never."

"Do you think it's him?"

"Look at it. It's got to be."

The door handle moved. I shut my eyes and tried to be ready. I tried to stop time. When they came back in they were altered, careful, like I was a bomb that might go off, a sleeping tiger, a priceless vase about to fall.

I thought they'd found me. I wondered how far I would get if I just ran.

Ginny's hand hovered over mine, without touching. Gordon tried to smile. I was terrified. Was this it?

"Cassiel?" she said.

I looked straight at her. I didn't know what was going on. "What?"

"Cassiel Roadnight?" she asked.

My name is not Cassiel Roadnight. It never has been. My name is Chap. That's what Grandad used to call me. I always thought it was a good name. I always thought it suited me.

"Who, *me?*" I said.

Gordon gave me the piece of paper. It was a printout, a picture of a boy with the word MISSING across his forehead.

A picture of me.

"Oh my God," I said, and I took in a breath and I held it.

It was old. I was about fourteen maybe, something like that.

Brown hair, not long and not short. Blue eyes, same shape, same lights and colors. My face exactly—my nose, my mouth, my chin.

I wondered if it was the last photo anyone had taken of me, and I wondered who took it.

I wondered why I was smiling. I didn't smile when I was fourteen. What did I have to smile about?

"Oh my God," I said again.

They misunderstood me. Ginny let her hand touch mine, and she squeezed. Gordon blew the air from his mouth with puffed cheeks, like a deflating ball. I kept my eyes on the picture.

There was something wrong with it.

Here are some things I know for sure about my face. I see them every time I look in the mirror. I know they are there without even having to look.

One. I have two scars. The first runs from my earlobe to my cheekbone, thin and raised and shiny, like one of the mends on my shirt. A dog bit me when I was five. It hurt like hell.

The second is beneath my left eye, a red mark, a swelling under my fingers, a diamond-shaped hole made by a boy with rings on every finger. I remember his face and I remember the sharp, weighted sound of those rings landing. His name was Rigg.

Two. I have three piercings in my left ear and two in my right. I did them myself with a needle and salt water and a cork. I breathed in deep and they didn't even bleed. There's nothing in them anymore, no studs or rings or whatever. I took them out, but the holes are still there. My ears look like pincushions.

Three. My teeth are bad. One at the front is broken, and three back ones are going to come out, even though they're supposed to last me a lifetime. My teeth are terrible.

In the picture there were no scars on my face, no piercings. I had perfect teeth. I was happy and well fed and wholesome.

In other words, it wasn't me.

I tried to tell them. I looked up from the picture and I said, "No."

"Cassiel," Gordon said. He crossed his legs. His trousers and his mouth made a shushing noise.

I shook my head. "Not me."

"Come on," Ginny said, her hand still on mine.

I wanted to swat it off. I didn't answer her.

"Whatever trouble you're in, Cassiel," she said, "whatever reason you had for running away, we can help you."

"No, you can't," I said. They were too close to me. I didn't like it.

"We're here to help," she said.

"Help someone else," I said. "Help someone who wants it. I'm not him."

"Who are you, then?" Gordon asked.

Good question.

I stared at him. I smiled my angriest smile.

"What are the odds," Gordon said to Ginny, like I wasn't

there, "of there being two *identical* missing boys?"

"*Billions* to one," Ginny said, like that settled it.

"I don't care what the odds are," I said. "It's not me."

"So what's your name, then?"

Maybe this is it, I thought. Just a trick to get me to tell them my name. I wasn't falling for it. They weren't going to find me. I'd managed to keep away from them for this long.

"It's not *Cassiel*," I said. "No way it's that."

They glanced at each other.

"Have another look," Gordon said.

And Ginny said, "Take your time."

They didn't believe me. They wanted to be right, I could tell that. They were going to insist on it. It doesn't matter what you say to people like that. When they have made up their minds, they stop listening.

I breathed in hard and tried not to think. I looked at the boy in the picture. I thought how incredible it was to have a double like that, somewhere out in the world, to look exactly like a total stranger. I looked at Cassiel Roadnight's happy, flawless, fearless face. And the thought occurred to me then, that I could be him if I wanted. It crept in. I could see it coming and I tried so hard not to notice it.

I *could* be.

And if I were Cassiel Roadnight, the thought said, I wouldn't have to be me anymore, whoever that was.

You won't exist, it said. *You could wipe yourself off the face of the earth in a second. You could vanish into thin air, right in front of your pursuers.*

I gave that thought my full attention. What did I have to lose?

There were people looking for Cassiel Roadnight, but they were people who cared. He had a family and friends. He had loved ones. He had a life I could step right into.

And what did I have?

Nobody. Nothing, except the fear of being found. The people looking for me just wanted to pull me apart.

I always wanted to be someone else. Doesn't everyone?

"Okay," I said to the thought, so quietly I almost didn't say it at all.

"What?" Gordon said.

They looked at each other and then back at me. It was like they'd been holding everything in. Suddenly there was this noise in the room of them breathing.

"Okay," I said.

"Good," said Ginny.

And Gordon said, "Your name is Cassiel Roadnight?"

"Yes," I told him. "My name is Cassiel Roadnight," and I watched the smile spread and stick to his face.

I lied. That's what I did wrong.

It didn't feel like much. Everybody lies once in a while. And just in case it counts in my defense, I wished it was the truth, I really did.

TWO

Ginny let me look myself up on the computer. She wasn't supposed to. Using the office equipment was against house rules. But then again, so was running, or having a knife that actually cut things, or eating a peanut.

"Just for a minute," she said, and she watched over my shoulder. I could smell her breath. I could hear her swallow.

I turned to look at her. "Do you want to leave me alone?"

There's no way she was allowed to do that. I watched her blink three times.

"Of course, Cassiel," she said, like she worked for me or something, like this was a hotel and I was paying to be there. "I'll be just down the hall."

God, having a name was something. Try being nobody and asking for your space.

Cassiel Roadnight had his own missing person's profile. He came from a small town where everybody knew him, where everybody knew each other. He went missing on fireworks night when the place was full of strangers, packed with people all come to see the procession and the dancing and the costumes and the fireworks and the Wicker Man. It happened every year. A celebration in the town, called Hay on Fire. It was a clever time to disappear.

It was the fifth of November. I looked at that date on the screen for a long time. Cassiel Roadnight hadn't been seen since then. Nor had I.

The profile said he was wearing jeans and a dark blue sweatshirt. His face was painted silver and gold for the procession, and over his ordinary clothes he wore a black cape and a mask that covered his eyes and nose. There were photos. It was strange to see a picture of him hours or maybe minutes before he was gone. It was even stranger to see my own eyes looking out from behind that mask.

His disappearance was "completely out of character," which means they didn't see it coming. He didn't leave a note, and he didn't tell anybody he was going.

His family said they would never give up hope of seeing him again.

They said, *"Cass, we miss you and think about you every day. There is no problem that we can't solve together. Just let us know that you are okay. And please come home."*

I would have liked a message like that. It would have meant a lot to me, people never giving up hope.

There were other photos of him too, not just the firework ones. I sat in the empty office and I looked at them all: Cassiel with an ice cream, Cassiel on the soccer team, Cassiel with a panting dog, Cassiel on a windswept beach. It was like looking at myself with a life I couldn't dream up, the life I wished I'd had. I knew I hadn't been there, I knew it wasn't true, but I willed myself to start hearing the drums in that procession, to start smelling the mud and sweat of the soccer field, to taste the strawberry pink of that ice cream, the salt and sand on my skin. I willed myself to start believing those pictures were pictures of me.

If you haven't eaten for a few days you have to be very careful to take little bites, or the food you've been wishing for and dreaming about day and night can make you worse than sick. Trust me, I know. That's why I knew not to wish for a family. I knew it was a terrible idea.

But wishing is addictive.

Cassiel Roadnight's life slipped into my head right then and stayed there. I couldn't make it go away. I thought about his mum and dad, about what they might look like, about how their faces would change when they saw me. I thought about his brothers and sisters, how many of them there might be, how old they were. I thought about his cozy little town and the gap he'd left by leaving. I thought about his friends. I imagined how happy they'd be when he came home.

I kidded myself that they needed me as much as I needed

them. I kidded myself I could end all their suffering just by showing up.

I thought about the kind of house Cassiel lived in, about his room and how it would feel when it was mine. I thought about breakfast at the table in the kitchen, pancakes and bad jokes and orange juice and the yellow sun on our faces. I thought about going to school and having friends and being normal.

I wished for what Cassiel Roadnight had. I wished with every single breath.

I didn't think about the knife-edge that being him would force me to live on. I failed to see it. I refused to look down.

I stared at his face on the computer screen and I dared myself to try it. Either I was going to make my wish come true, or I had to go right now and tell Gordon and Ginny the truth. I could become him, or I had to become me. That was my choice.

I picture it often, me walking down the corridor toward them, pretending to choose. I replay the scene in my head, the time just before there was no going back, the last seconds I was no one, not me and not Cassiel Roadnight yet, not quite.

My shoes squeak on the polished floor, my hands feel hot and swollen and clammy, and I think I am undecided. I think I don't know what I'm going to do.

Undecided seems like a magical place to me now, a place before action and consequence.

Undecided is what I wish for.

•   •   •

I knocked on the door. Gordon and Ginny were making phone calls. They'd been talking to the police and missing persons and social services. They were all coffee and triumph and activity. My lie had snowballed into fact already while my back was turned.

"Cassiel, my *man*," Gordon said, wheeling his chair away from his desk. "How're you doing?"

It was embarrassing, him talking like that. I knew it and he knew it. I looked at him and he looked away.

"It's Cass," I said. "That's what people call me."

I didn't know I was going to say it, but when it came out it sounded right. I liked the feeling of the name in my voice. I was tall and I looked down on Gordon in his chair. I had a family and friends and somewhere to be. I was somebody. The fugitive I'd been had finally disappeared.

Nobody could get me now.

"Sorry," he said, clearing his throat. "Cass. What can we do for you?"

I said I'd finished on the computer.

"Good lad," he said, straightening himself. "Find what you were looking for?"

I shrugged. (Yes Yes Yes. I'd found everything I ever wanted.)

I said, "What happens next?"

Ginny said that they were arranging for my family to be told. She said, "Someone will let them know as soon as possible.

Then we can sort out getting you home."

Home.

I didn't know what to look at. A kind of hunger burst open in my gut, this cool empty space. I licked my lips, and I felt a sudden fine sheen of sweat rise in my hair and under my arms.

Gordon said, "It won't be long now."

I heard what he said and I didn't hear it at the same time. I think I nodded.

Home. Was it that easy?

Ginny said, "You do want to go home, don't you, Cassiel? Is that what you want to do?"

"Yes," I said. "I want it more than anything in the world."

I thought she might laugh. The whole world could have burst out laughing right then and I wouldn't have been surprised. Who was I to want anything?

"Well, good," Ginny said. "Of course you do."

Gordon sat back in his chair with his hands behind his head, and because the conversation seemed to be over, I left the room. I put one foot in front of the other, and when I got out I leaned against the wall and shut my eyes and made my heart slow down just by asking it to.

I was him.

And with each step I took as Cassiel Roadnight, with each new slowing heartbeat, I replaced something I wanted to forget about having been me.

THREE

My grandad's place was a big house that backed on to the park. I don't remember anything before that. I've tried. Through the window I could see the playground, kids moving all over it like ants on a dropped lollipop.

Being in that house was like going back in time. It was quiet and dark and book-lined and mostly brown, full of clocks ticking, real clocks counting the days away in every room. The curtains were always closed, as though outside didn't matter. Grandad thought the best thing a person could spend his day doing was reading in the dark. I don't think it ever crossed his mind that not everybody wanted to do it.

After the accident, people kept saying it was no place for a child, the health visitors and social workers and neighbors and noseyeffingparkers, as Grandad would've called them.

They didn't ask me. It didn't matter what I thought.

There were thirteen rooms in that house. I counted them. Grandad only lived in one.

I thought he must have used them once, must have needed them for something, like a wife and kids or dogs or lodgers or whatever it was he had before he had me. He never talked about it, even if I asked him. He acted like there wasn't anything to remember before there was him and me. He called it The Time Before, and that's all he'd say about it.

Grandad was happiest just to sit and read and sleep and drink in the front room, the one with the big bay window you couldn't ever see out of. Sometimes he got up and shuffled out to the bathroom or the kitchen or to get the mail off the doormat, but not all that often. Sometimes he ventured out to the shop on the corner and shuffled back again, bottles clinking, whiskers glinting, hair gone wild.

We had our bed in the front room by the fire, and his chair, and his books, and his bottles. It was warm in there, not like the rest of the house, which was so cold your face felt it first, as soon as you went out there, then your fingers and the tip of your nose died just a little. Those were my places: the weed–run garden, the other twelve rooms, and the arctic upstairs, lifeless like a museum or a film set; a perfect timepiece, fallen into quiet and fascinating ruin.

In the stifling warmth of the front room I'd run my hands over the wallpaper that felt like flattened rope. The pattern of the curtains looked like radioactive chocolates in a box. That's what I always thought when I looked at them. Chocolates of the future. Chocolates you should never ever eat. I couldn't imagine Grandad choosing those curtains. I often wondered who did.

I slept in there with Grandad every night. I made a nest of cushions at the end of the bed. He sat in his sagging leather chair and read to me, with the bottle on the table at his side so he wouldn't have to stop for it. He read me H. G. Wells and John Wyndham. He read me C. S. Lewis and Charles Dickens and Tolkien and *Huckleberry Finn*. Every night he read until I was asleep on my cushions or he was asleep in his chair. That's how we said good night, by disappearing in the middle of a sentence.

And that's how I learned everything I know, with the clocks' soft ticking and the heating *click-click* of the gas fire and the raised nap of velvet against my cheek and the smell of whiskey and the sound of Grandad's voice reading.

How could that not be a place for a child?

How could they say that?

What did they know?

FOUR

The next day I got a phone call.

Ginny came running down the corridor to find me. I was picking at a hole in my jeans. I was waiting. I was trying to take time apart minute by minute, second by second. It wasn't working.

Ginny had sweat across her upper lip. It glistened. "Cassiel," she said. "It's for you. It's your sister."

I walked behind her, back the way she had come. When we got to the office I looked at the receiver for a moment before I picked it up. Ginny flapped with her hands and mouthed at me to talk.

"Hello?" I said.

"Cass?"

He had a sister.

I could tell how hard she was shaking, by her voice. I wanted to make her stop.

I looked at Ginny. She was still flapping. I turned my back on her.

"Cass. It's Edie."

"Hello, Edie."

She made a little sound, not a whole word really, and then she said, "Is that you?"

"Yes," I said. "It's me."

Then I sat in the office with my eyes closed, and I listened to this Edie girl I'd never met crying because I was alive. I'd imagined people jumping around, beside themselves with joy and relief, not sobbing miles away on the end of the phone. I didn't think it would be like that.

When she stopped crying, when she talked, I pretended it was *me* she was talking to, me she'd been missing all this time, me she was so happy to have found. I pretended she was my sister. That way I didn't have to feel so bad.

She said, "I'm coming to get you, Cass. Please stay where you are. Please don't disappear again before I get there."

"Okay."

"You promise?"

"I promise."

"Oh God. Mum's not here. I can't get hold of her. I'm just going to come. I'll be there. Don't move!"

"I won't move," I said. "I'll wait here."

She took a long time to say good-bye. I put the phone down and forced myself to smile at Ginny.

22

"Well?" she said, "How was that?"

I didn't know why she was asking. She'd heard all she needed, hanging around by the photocopier, pretending to be busy, holding herself still so she could listen.

"Good," I said.

"You didn't say much," she said.

"I never do."

I went to my room and sat on my bed. The dinner bell sounded and the soccer on TV started and the showers were free, but I just stayed there.

I should have run away. I should have got out of it while I still could. But I didn't go anywhere. I didn't get off my bed even. I didn't leave the room. I didn't move. Because suddenly I had a sister, and she'd told me not to.

Four hours later, I heard Edie before I saw her. I heard her walking toward my room, and my stomach opened up like a canyon. Her shoes clapped gently next to Gordon's and Ginny's wheezy, squeaking steps.

When they came in, she stopped and put her hands up over her mouth. She stood there with Ginny beaming behind her.

I didn't know what to do with my face.

I could feel a big flashing sign above my head that said THIS IS NOT HIM. I waited for her to notice it. I waited for her to say, "You're not my brother," and I thought about what would happen next. Would sirens start wailing? Would I melt like candle wax into a puddle on the floor? How many people would hit me? Where would they put me, once they knew?

And if she thought I was Cassiel? If she fitted me into his place like the wrong piece in a puzzle, what would happen then? I was more scared of that than anything. And I wanted it more than anything too.

I stood there and waited for her to decide.

She kept her hands over her mouth. Her makeup bled from her eyes onto her skin. I thought about her putting mascara on that morning, before she knew she was going to see her missing brother.

"Say something, Cassiel," whispered Ginny.

She said it like I was an idiot, like I was four years old. I wanted to hit her.

"Hello, Edie," I said. My voice didn't sound like mine.

Edie took a deep breath and she got Ginny and Gordon to leave us on our own. She didn't speak, she just asked them with her eyes and her hands, and they said yes.

And then I was alone with her. And suddenly I knew that anything I did, just one tiny thing, a word, a look, a gesture, could blow this open, could scream the house down that I wasn't him. I was a cell under the microscope. She was the all-seeing eye. I couldn't breathe. I couldn't move. I stood dead still and I watched her.

She wasn't what I'd been expecting. She was a lot smaller

than me, and her hair was long and dark. Long dark hair and blue eyes overflowing with water and light, a smile so full of sadness, it made me feel grateful to have seen it, like a rare flower.

"Talk to me," she said.

I had to clear my throat. My voice was shrunken, hiding. "What about?"

She shrugged and her eyes ran and she didn't say anything, not for a bit. She just looked at me. The asking and relief on her face made me flinch. It was like staring at the sun.

After a while she looked at the floor and said, "I don't believe it. I can't take this in."

I breathed out. I just watched her. I didn't know what else to do.

"It's really you?" she said.

I nodded. My tongue felt swollen and dry in my mouth. I needed a drink of water.

"Say something," she said. "Why aren't you saying anything?"

Because I'm scared to. Because you don't know me. Because I'll say the wrong thing.

"It's good to see you," I said.

"Good?" she said. "*Good?* Two years, Cass. You have to do better than *good*."

"Sorry."

"I drove so fast," she said. "I kept thinking I was going to

25

crash. I thought I was going to turn the car over, but I couldn't slow down.

"Where have you *been*?" she said. "Why didn't you call? What the hell happened to you?"

My lips were stuck together. Somebody had sewn my mouth shut.

"You've changed so much," she said.

I felt the dusting of stubble over my chin. I rubbed my fingers across my cheeks, through my overgrown hair. I ran my tongue over my bad teeth.

"You too," I said. Could I say that? Was that wrong?

"You are so tall."

"Am I?"

"Why did you leave?" she said suddenly, and the skin of her voice broke, the anguish welling up underneath. "Why did you do that?"

"I'm sorry," I said.

"I thought you were *dead*," she said. "People said you were dead."

"I'm not dead."

She nodded again and her face caved in, and she cried, proper crying, all water and snot. She couldn't catch her breath. She stood on the other side of the room and looked at me like she wanted me to make it better. I didn't know what to do. I waited for her to stop, but she crossed the room and walked right into me. She cried all over my shirt.

While she did it I shut my eyes and breathed slowly.

I had a sister and she was perfect and she cared that I was there.

I think it was the closest to happy I'd ever been. And I knew I was going to hell for it.

I know it still. If there's a hell, that's where I'll go.

FIVE

Now and again I persuaded Grandad that we needed to go out—to the city farm maybe, or the market, or along the canal. He never saw the point. I think after years of hiding in the dust-yellow insides of his books, real life was like roping lead weights to his feet and jumping into cold water; just not something he felt like doing.

He didn't mind me going out on my own. He said it was a good idea.

He said, "The namby-pamby children of today have no knowledge of danger and no sense of direction."

He said, "When I was your age I was out for days at a time with nothing but a compass and a piece of string."

He said he very much doubted I'd get lost or stolen, or fall down a manhole.

He was right. I didn't.

Still, sometimes I persuaded him to get dressed and come

with me, just because I liked him being there, just because he needed the fresh air. His skin was lightless and thin like paper. His hair was like a burned cloud. I told him if he didn't get out in the sunshine once in a while, he might turn into a page from one of his mildewed books, and the slightest gust of wind would blow him to nothing. I sort of believed it.

Out on my own I was quick and agile. I could walk on walls and weave through crowds and duck under bridges and squeeze into tiny spaces and jump over gates. Grandad wasn't so good at walking. He stumbled a lot, and staggered sometimes, and forgot where he was going. Once he fell into the canal. Not fell, exactly—he was too close to the edge and he walked right into it, like it was what he'd been meaning to do all along. He was wearing a big sheepskin coat, and it got all heavy with water, and he couldn't get up again. It wasn't deep, it wasn't dangerous. It was funny. He stood there with the filthy water up to his chest, soaking into his coat, changing the color of it from sand to black.

"Come on in," he said to me. "The water's lovely."

"No thanks, Grandad," I said.

He winked at me. "This reminds me," he said, trying to heave himself up off the bottom, "of my childhood vacations on the French Riviera."

I think the coat weighed more than he did. He took it off, in the end, and waded out in his thin suit, like a wet dog. The coat lay there on the water, like a man facedown with his arms stretched out on either side, looking for something on the canal floor, quietly drowning. We had to rescue it with a stick.

"I never liked this coat," Grandad said as we walked back the way we'd come, carrying it between us like a body, straight back to the house. His teeth banged together when he talked, like an old skeleton. Water ran off him like a wet tent. His shoes were ruined. There were leaves in his hair, leaves and rat shit.

We laughed and laughed.

I didn't know Grandad was drunk then. It never occurred to me. I don't think I knew what drunk was. When you're a kid you fall over and bang into things all the time. I didn't realize you were supposed to grow out of it.

I wouldn't have minded anyway. If you ask me, Grandad drunk wasn't any worse than Grandad sober. Not when you love a person that much. Not when a person is all you've got.

I only saw Grandad cry one time, and he hadn't been drinking. He hadn't been allowed to. It was after the accident, when I went to see him, just that once.

He was so pale, so almost lifeless, I thought he was disappearing.

He tried to talk to me. He tried to tell me the truth, and his tears kept getting in the way of the words. Great racking sobs tore through his voice.

I didn't hold him like I held Edie. I was too shocked.

I should have held him like I held her. I should have done it, but I didn't.

SIX

Suddenly I was free to leave. Edie signed some papers to say she was responsible for me. She showed Gordon her driver's license to prove she was over eighteen and who she said she was—Cassiel's big sister and all that.

She came with me to get my things. I'd packed them in my rucksack, and it was waiting on my bed.

There wasn't much. A flashlight without batteries, a knife and fork I'd lifted from the canteen, a tennis ball, a pencil, a kingfisher feather, an empty wallet, an old notebook, some postcards, a pair of jeans, two ancient shirts, and a sweatshirt I'd found on a railing.

I found my rucksack in a Dumpster, years ago. There was a slash down one side and one of the straps was broken, so it got dumped. All I did was tape it up and tie a knot in it, and it worked fine. It's amazing what you can find if you're looking. Perfectly good things get thrown away all the time, perfectly good things and perfectly good people.

"Is that yours?" Edie said.

I nodded.

"What have you got?"

"Not much."

She reached out and took it before I could stop her. I watched her unzip it. All I could think was there might be something in there with my name on it, something just waiting to give me away, but there wasn't. My stuff looked like it had just washed up there, in the torn black inside. It looked like stuff the sea had spat out.

"I don't recognize any of this," she said.

I shrugged. "I guess not."

She picked out the tiny, blue-streaked feather. "Can I have it?" she said.

"Okay."

"It's funny," she said, brushing the fine tip of it with her fingers.

"What is?"

"That you've been missing and a thing like this has been with you all this time."

We walked outside to her car, an old silver Peugeot with a dent in its flank and one almost flat tire. There were plastic flowers hanging from her rearview mirror, a load of old newspapers on the back shelf. They swelled like sails and snapped shut when we opened and closed the doors.

I wondered how Cassiel Roadnight got into a car. I wondered if the way I did it might give me away.

Gordon and Ginny and a few of the boys stood in the front yard, waiting for us to go so they could get on with whatever happened next. Nobody knew what to say.

"Good luck." Gordon had his head half through the open car window. I thought about winding it shut with his face still in it. I thought about just driving away.

"Thank you *so* much," Edie said. "I don't know how to thank you."

Ginny said to me, "Let us know how you're getting on." But she didn't mean it, and she knew I wouldn't.

"Okay," Edie said, looking at her feet and then at me, starting the car, pulling it around in reverse. "Let's go."

We turned on to the road, and the house and everyone in it were suddenly gone, as if they never existed. I thought for a second that maybe I'd been safer there, maybe I'd been better off. For a second I wished she'd just take me back and leave me. Now, rather than later. Now, before everyone got hurt too much.

The car was small and messy and crowded. A fallen-over basket had spilled its stuff on the floor, and a big blue bag took up most of the room at my feet. There were clothes all over the backseat. The dashboard was covered in flyers and scraps of paper and parking tickets. It stank of incense. I was sitting on something. I reached underneath myself and pulled it out—a piece of old knitted blanket, just a scrap, gray with dirt and dotted with holes. I'd have guessed she used it to clean the windscreen, if the windscreen had ever been cleaned. I was about to drop it. It was the look on Edie's face that stopped me. Instead I held it in my hand for a minute, pushed my fingers through its loops and swirls.

Edie watched me.

Was this how hard it was to be someone else? Did I have to be this vigilant? How long was I going to last, when even a scrap of filth might turn out to be something special?

Edie straightened in her seat, took a deep breath, smiled at the road.

"I thought you might have missed it," she said. "I know you're too old for it and everything. I just thought it would make you smile."

"Thanks," I said. I smiled, on cue. It felt like my face was splitting open. I put the rag in my rucksack.

It was good being in a place without lockers and filing cabinets and industrial cleaning fluid and a place for everything. I watched Edie's hands on the steering wheel. She had a gold ring on the little finger of her right hand, a silver one on the middle of her left. The veins were raised and faintly blue beneath her skin, thin fine bones rippling with each small movement. It was hot in the car, hot and dry. The air blew in through the heaters and leeched the moisture from my eyes and mouth. While she drove, Edie looked straight ahead and in her mirrors and at her shoulder and over at me.

"I'm going to drive slowly on the way home," she said. "I'm not going to crash or turn the car over."

"Okay," I said. And inside, I heard a part of me wishing that she would.

For a long time we didn't say anything. The quiet in the car was full of us not knowing what to say.

I thought about where we were going and what it would be like and who was waiting there. I thought about how the hell I was ever going to get away with it. Every time I thought about it, my body opened out like it was hollow, like forgetting something vital, like knowing you're in trouble, like waking up to nothing but regret.

"We're very quiet," she said, "for people with two years of stories to tell."

I liked it, being quiet. I couldn't make a mistake if I was quiet.

"There's no rush, is there?" I said.

"I suppose not," she said. "I suppose we never talked that much before."

She changed gear and it didn't go in right, and the car grated and squealed until she got it.

"I missed you, Cass," she said.

What was I supposed to say to that? I looked at my feet. I looked out the window. She was still missing him. She hadn't stopped, poor thing. She just didn't know it.

"I dreamed about you," she said.

What would he have said to that? Thank you? Sorry?

"In my head you were the same as when you left," she said. "I expected you to look the same." She almost smiled. "It's been two years. It's stupid."

We drove past a pub called The Homecoming. It looked warm inside, and noisy. I thought myself out of the car and into the pub, taking people's drinks when their backs were turned. I saw myself through the windows.

"I wonder if Mum and Frank have got my messages," she said. "I couldn't get hold of them."

I didn't know who these people were. I didn't have the slightest idea of what to say.

"They might not know yet," she said. "How weird is that?"

I could see her searching my eyes for something that wasn't there. I blinked, and so did she.

"God, Cassiel," she said. "I can't believe it's you."

I knew exactly what she meant, even if she didn't.

SEVEN

Think of the perfect cottage, right at the end of a lane that lifts and drops through woodland and runs high along the ridges of fields. A white picket fence, a covered porch grown thick with quince and scented roses, a garden alive with birdsong, and the quiet constant thrum of a stream.

I am not making this up. I didn't dream it or read about it. This place exists. It's where Edie took me.

Home.

I pretended to fall asleep in the seat next to her, so I wouldn't have to worry about what to say. I let my eyes give in and close, and I stayed at the small center of myself, listening. I listened to the engine and the tick of the turn signal and to Edie breathing. I listened to the air outside the windows and the rush-rush of other cars and the music she put on, turned down low so it wouldn't wake me.

I listened when she answered her phone. It rang once.

A woman's voice, high and thin and tinny, said, *"Is it him?"* I heard her say it.

"It's him," Edie said, and I knew she was looking at me while she said it. "It's Cass."

"Oh my God," the voice said, loud.

"He's right next to me. Asleep," Edie said. "Perfect. Tall."

Edie nudged me. I shifted in my seat and stretched. She nudged me again, harder. I opened my eyes and looked at the moving sweep of buildings and lampposts and trees. None of them knew the terrible lie I'd started; none of them cared.

Edie held out the phone to me like a question. I shrank from it. I shook my head. She held it out again, harder. She put it in my hand.

"It's Mum."

"Hello?" I said.

Breathing rattled out of Edie's phone, shallow and ragged. It made me think of a long-distance runner, of a sick dog.

She didn't say anything.

"Hello?"

"Who's that?" she said. "Is it you?"

She heard the lie in my voice. A mother would. She would know straight away. I spoke away from the mouthpiece so I'd be harder to hear. "Yes, it's me."

Then the weeping, just like with Edie. The strange small noise and the empty feeling of listening to it. I looked at Edie. I gave her back the phone.

"Mum," she said. "It's over. He's coming home."

Nothing. More sobbing. I thought I heard her say, "Are you sure?"

"Got to go. We'll be there in a couple of hours."

Edie let the phone drop into her lap. "You okay?" she said.

I tried to keep my eyes on the running gray of the road ahead. I liked the way I had to keep them moving just to stay looking at the same place.

"I'm fine," I said.

I wanted to find out where we were going. I wanted to ask how long it would take, but I couldn't. I was supposed to know.

"What are you thinking about?" she said.

I hate that question. If you're thinking about it, it's private. If you wanted someone else to know, you'd speak.

"Home," I said.

She straightened in her seat, looped a strand of hair behind her ear. "I have to tell you something," she said.

"What?"

"You're not going to like it."

"Okay."

She looked over at me. She spoke too fast. "Please don't be cross. Please don't mind. Frank bought us a house. We moved."

It took me a minute to work a few things out.

I didn't mind. For me this was good news. For me it was a gift.

Edie was holding herself away from me, waiting for a reaction. I couldn't tell if it was me that made her nervous, or her brother; the person she didn't know or the one she did.

Cassiel was missing. Wasn't his family supposed to wait for him? Weren't his loved ones supposed to be right there when he made it home? I pictured him making the journey, knocking on the door to a houseful of strangers, doubly abandoned. Cassiel would mind.

"That's harsh," I said. I shook my head.

"It wasn't up to me," she said, not looking at me, keeping her eyes on her mirrors, keeping her face toward the road.

"Whose idea was it?"

I listened to myself sounding bothered. I marveled at my own hypocrisy.

Edie spoke too fast. "Frank found it," she said. "He thought it was the best thing for Mum, you know. Give her something else to think about."

"Right."

"It was her dream house. Remember the one we always used to walk past on our way up to the common? It was up for sale and Frank's been doing really well and . . ."

"That was nice of him," I said.

Who the hell was Frank? A rich uncle? Their dad? Their mum's boyfriend?

"Yes," Edie said, smiling. "It was."

She put her hand on mine, and we drove along like that for a while, with me looking at our hands, and her looking at the road.

"I thought you'd be angry," she said.

"Do you want me to be?"

"No," she said. "God, no. I just thought you would be, that's all. You've every right."

It made me smile, the idea that I was entitled to anything.

"It's done," I said. "I don't see the point."

I shut my eyes again, and for a while I slept for real. I dreamed I was looking at my face in the mirror. I was wondering how the hell I'd ended up looking like I did.

It was the killing of the engine that woke me again, the lack of sound, and then the slam of Edie's door. I opened my eyes, alone on a dirt track surrounded by nothing but green. It was getting dark. It was unreal, like waking from one dream into another. I'd never been in that much space before. The wind blew across the land and straight at me, like now that I was there it had something to aim for. I could hear it singing through and over and under the car. For less than a second I wondered if Edie had left me there, if she'd worked it out and abandoned me. And then I heard the creak of a gate and she was back, striding through the sheer emptiness, opening and closing the door, bringing a little piece of the gale and the smell of cold grass in with her.

"Welcome home, Cass," she said.

The car stumbled through the open gate, slicing through wet mud and tractor marks. Edie got out to shut it again behind us. The green plain narrowed into a tree-lined path, and then there it was. Cassiel's mother's dream house. There was a light on downstairs and it spilled out warm and yellow into the air. Edie beeped the horn twice, and the front door flung open. It wasn't until the porch light snapped on that I saw her properly, thin and dark and windblown, an older version of Edie, just as fragile-looking, just as small. She put her hands to her mouth the same as Edie did when she first saw me. Then she was jumping and waving, her shouts vanishing into the wind. She ran at the car. I watched her close in on us like a tornado, like water. There was no escaping her.

Edie stared at me. "What's wrong?" she said. "You look like you're going to be *sick*."

"Nothing."

"You're scared. What are you scared of?"

I didn't have time to answer. Cassiel's mother was on us, on me. She wrenched open the door with both hands. The wind grabbed my hair and filled my ears, and she tried to pull me straight out by my arms and throw herself on me at the same time.

I heard Edie get out of the car on the other side, free and unnoticed, like she was invisible, like she wasn't there. I saw myself suddenly from the outside, in this wind-racked, mud-filled place, pretending to be this woman's son. I couldn't breathe.

Wouldn't she know? Wouldn't she know as soon as she touched me?

Cassiel's mother had bangles that clanked and rang, and her nails were bitten so hard, so far down, I couldn't look at them. I tried to get out of the car with her still clinging to me. I tried to stand up.

"My boy," she said, and then she pulled me into the crook of her neck, my forehead on her shoulder, my back bent over like a scythe. Her clothes smelled of the warm inside, of dog and log fires and cooking, of cigarette smoke. I felt her breathing, thin and weak, like she was worn out from years of doing the same. She laughed into my hair and tightened her thin arms across my back. Her breath smelled of flowers and ash.

I stored it in a quiet and empty place in my mind. So this was what a mum felt like.

Cassiel's mother drew back to look at me. Her eyes were wild and triumphant, and at the dark center of them there was something like fear. I tried not to let her see how scared *I* was. I listened to the countdown in my head that ended with her disappointed scream.

It didn't come. I got to zero and she hadn't let go.

"I never thought I'd see you again," she said, shaking her head, the threat of tears drowning her voice. "I never thought I'd see you."

She grabbed my shirt, my mended charity-shop shirt, like she thought her hand might go straight through it. "You're real." She whispered it.

"Yes."

"You came back."

"Yes."

I don't know how long we stood there, in that wet, freezing air. She rocked, as if she were holding a baby, but it was me holding her up, I think. Edie had gone in. A dog came out onto the porch, sniffed the air, stretched its back legs, and went in again. My car door was still open and the light was on inside. I worried briefly about the battery. The trees thrashed wildly at the house, as if they knew there was something to be angry about, as if they knew what wrong was being committed there. I glared at them, and they thrashed wildly at me too.

When the phone rang inside the house, Cassiel's mother jumped, like she'd been sleeping, or miles away.

"That'll be Frank," she said. She wiped her eyes and smoothed her hair back, like whoever Frank was, he'd be able to see her. "Let's go in," she said. "Let's talk to Frank."

She took my hand to walk with me, but when I pulled back to get my bag and shut the car door, she didn't wait. She let go and went ahead to the house and left me there for a moment in the wind and the dark, alone.

• • •

Inside, the house was warm and smelled of cinnamon and onions and wood smoke. Underneath the wood smoke there was something cloying and rotten, like garbage cans, like decay.

It was horribly bright. I felt the light fall on each line and hollow of my face that was different to Cassiel's. I felt my face change, looming and hideous in its strangeness. I saw my reflection in the mirror. I was me, not him. Wasn't it obvious?

Edie and her mother weren't looking, not really. They can't have been. But they might at any moment. I stood still and waited for that moment to come.

I looked around me at the kitchen, low-ceilinged with a black slate floor and bloodred cupboards, an old stove pumping out heat, a long scrubbed table down the middle. There was a sofa against the wall, torn and scruffy, with old velvet cushions that for a split second made me think of Grandad.

The dog was in his basket in the corner. He didn't get up. He lifted his eyes, wagged his tail at us lazily, *thump-thump-thump* on the floor. He was a wiry mongrel of a thing, old and coarse and graying. I scratched his neck, read the name *Sergeant* on his collar. He rolled over and exposed the bald pink of his tummy, the upside-down spread of his smile.

Cassiel's mother was flushed from the cold air, her knuckles bone-white where she gripped the phone.

"Is that Frank?" I said.

Edie nodded. "He just got our messages."

Cassiel's mother held the phone out to me. "Cass," she said.

"Come and speak to Frank. Let your big brother hear your voice."

I took the phone out of her hand, and she stroked the side of my face. I looked her in the eye. I waited for her to notice.

"Hello, Frank," I said, and stood still and obedient while she stroked me.

Frank was smoking. I could hear the wet suck of him pulling on a cigarette, the thickened taking in of breath. He laughed, and in my mind I saw his mouth and all the smoke pouring from it.

"Cass," he said. "You're home." His voice was low and warm.

"Yes," I said.

He sounded calm and confident. I liked the sound of him. "I can't wait to see you," he said.

"Me too."

"I'm coming straight home."

"When. Tonight?"

"In the morning."

"Okay. Good. Thanks."

Would it be him that saw it? Would he look at his brother and see the liar underneath?

"It's a miracle, Cass," Frank said, his mouth close to the phone, his lips brushing against the mouthpiece as he spoke, so the sound of him grazed my ears.

"Not really," I said.

"No, believe me," Frank was saying. "*You* are a miracle."

Cassiel's mother was holding her hand out for the phone. "Mum wants you," I said.

"No. Tell Helen I've got to go," he said. "Tell her I'll see her tomorrow."

"Okay."

"And, Cass," he said.

"Yes?"

"Welcome home."

He put the phone down. I listened for a moment to the empty line.

I had a big brother now too.

Helen. Cassiel's mum's name was Helen. Was that what Cassiel called her? Or did he call her Mum? She was standing so close to me. She could have counted my eyelashes from where she was standing. She didn't seem to notice my scars, the old holes in my ears, the thousand other differences there must be. Didn't she see me?

"He's gone," I said.

The focus of her eyes slipped a little, but she kept them on me. I watched them go. I watched them loosen and fade and come back, her pupils lost in clouded, muddied blue, her gaze slack. Cassiel's mother was high. She didn't see me at all.

Edie was watching me. I wondered if she saw the shock on

my face. I wondered if I was supposed to know.

Helen sat down at the table, smiled at nothing, started rolling a cigarette.

Edie picked my bag up and opened the door to a dark hallway. "Are you coming?" she asked me.

"Where?" Helen said.

"I was going to give him a tour. He doesn't know where anything is."

They spoke *about* Cassiel, even though I was standing right in front of them. I supposed that's just what they were used to, Cassiel getting talked about, Cassiel not being there. I supposed it was fitting, in a way.

Edie looked at me. "Do you want to?"

"Yes," I said. "Yes, I do."

In the dark hallway she opened a door to the stairs. She held my bag in her hand, low by the strap, and dropped it on the bottom step. The banisters were wood, painted a pale bluish gray. The steps were dusty, dancing with fluff and crumbs, dots of paper, and scraps of tobacco.

"Did you like the kitchen?" she said.

"It's nice," I said. "Pretty."

She smiled. Her teeth and the whites of her eyes were like stone in the dark. "Not words I'm used to hearing you say."

Did I have to be that careful? Did the words *pretty* and *nice* betray me? I was trying to be a good boy. I was trying to be like him, that's all.

"What's in here?" I said, walking through a space on my right. It was a little room with boots and coats and a load of boxes.

"Not much," Edie said, turning away, opening a door opposite. "This one's the sitting room."

There was a big low fireplace and a glass chandelier, three battered armchairs, and a thick rug on the floor. It was cold.

"We hardly ever go in here," Edie said. "It's nicer in the kitchen."

She took me upstairs. She pulled the door to the stairway shut behind us. Her voice echoed between the narrow walls. "Why did you look so surprised?" she said.

"When?"

"When you looked at Mum."

I tried to think.

"Do you think she's worse?" Edie said.

I shrugged. "Hard to say."

"She gets them off the Internet now," Edie said.

"What?"

"Valium. Xanax. God knows. The doctor wouldn't give her enough anymore. He was telling her to stop."

"Maybe she should."

Edie looked hard at me for a second. "You never thought that before," she said.

Damn. "Didn't I?"

She took the last bend in the stairs. "What did you call them? Mummy managers."

I tried to smile. "Oh, yeah."

"Keep her half tuned out so she doesn't care what you're up to. Ring a bell?"

It was even colder up there, and our feet were loud on the wooden floor.

"You and Frank both," she said. "You're as bad as each other."

Cassiel's room was the third door on the right after Frank's room and the bathroom. Across the hallway were Helen's and Edie's.

Edie went into Cassiel's room before me, strolled right in like it was no big deal. Dust swarmed in the light from the ceiling. I thought about breathing it in. I thought about it swarming like that inside my nose and mouth and throat and lungs.

I stopped in the doorway like the air itself was pushing me away. It wasn't my room. It wasn't my stuff to touch.

"What?" Edie said.

I looked past her. "Nothing."

"Is it different?" she said. "I tried to make it look exactly the same."

I said, "I'm just looking."

The dust swarmed harder and faster around me when I walked in, like it was angry. Here was his mother holding me tight, here was his sister asking me in. But even the dust in Cassiel's room knew I wasn't him.

"It's tidier," she said. "You can't miss that."

I looked at his stuff. I moved around the room, picking things up, touching them, opening drawers. A mirror with an apple printed on it, a skin drum, a picture of two banjo players in a small metal frame. A book about mask-making, a folder of drawings, a skateboard. A stack of postcards, a laptop, a poster for a film I'd never heard of. Clothes, washed and ironed and folded and waiting for someone to wear them for two whole years. They were way too small for me. They'd never fit him now.

I thought about Cassiel watching me from somewhere, from a daydream, from a park bench, from a checkout, from heaven or hell or the plain cold grave, wherever he might be.

I wondered how much he would hate me for what I was doing.

I wondered when he was coming to get me back.

"Does it feel weird?" she said.

"A bit," I said.

"Yeah," she said. "I've got this running commentary in my head: *My little brother's home.*"

She sounded like an announcer at a railway station. "*My little brother is home and in his room.*"

No, he's not, the commentary in my head said. *No, he isn't.*

"Do you like it?" she said. "Do you like your room?"

I didn't answer. She didn't notice.

"It's bigger than the old one, isn't it? Do you like the color? It's called Lamp Room Gray or something. Mum said it was boring. I think it's cool."

I smiled.

"You hate it," she said.

"I don't."

Helen came upstairs and knocked on the open door. Edie took her eyes off me for a moment to look at her.

"You are so tall," Helen said.

"Am I?"

"I forgot you'd be two years older." She leaned on the doorframe. She crossed her arms around herself and watched me.

"I said the same thing," Edie said. "It's like you grew in five minutes."

Helen nodded. "It's a lot to take in."

When she blinked, she blinked slowly, like her eyes would have been happy staying closed.

"Where have you been, Cassiel?"

"What happened? Tell us what happened."

They spoke at the same time, almost. They were nothing but questions. I couldn't answer them. My disguise was paper-thin. I didn't know who Cassiel Roadnight was or what he'd say. If I spoke, I'd eat away at it, I'd just show myself lurking underneath, the rotten core.

"Not now," I said.

"When?" Edie said.

"Leave it, love," said Helen.

It was quiet, tense, like a standoff. I could hear us all breathing. I thought about how big Cassiel's breaths were, how many times a minute his heart beat.

"Are you hungry?" Helen said.

I should be. I don't think I'd eaten since Edie called. But I wasn't. My stomach was like a closed fist. There was too much to think about. Too much could go wrong.

Cassiel would be. He would be relaxed and hungry and tired. Cassiel was home.

"I think so," I said.

"Good. Let's eat."

They left the room ahead of me, and I listened to them go along the landing and down the stairs. I stopped in the doorway and looked back into his room. The dust was still frenzied in the light from the bulb. I switched it off.

The dust disappeared, just like that.

EIGHT

I never ate meat in my life before I was Cassiel Roadnight. Not once.

According to Grandad, being a vegetarian wasn't just about health or cruelty or money or flavor; it was also about manners. He said that stealing milk and eggs and honey was enough of a liberty without hacking off someone's leg and then drowning it in gravy. He had a point.

He taught me how to cook. He trusted me with all the sharp knives and all the boiling water I could get my hands on. We ate rice and beans and vegetables. We ate a lot of curry. We ate like kings.

That's what Grandad used to say.

After the accident, when I wasn't allowed to see Grandad anymore, they tried to make me eat meat. They put withered, puckered, stinking things on my plate and told me if I didn't eat them there'd be trouble. They said they were good for me.

They didn't know the first thing about what was good for me.

I told them that. I screamed it in their faces. I said I didn't eat meat. I said I wanted my Grandad. I threw the food at them. I threw it at the walls and the windows and their faces. I threw it anywhere it wanted to land. I didn't eat their meat. I didn't do it.

I'd rather have starved.

Cassiel's favorite food was meatballs. Helen put a plateful down in front of me, and it was clear from the look on her face that meatballs were something I was supposed to get all excited and nostalgic about.

"Meatballs," I said. "Thanks."

Edie said, "How many times have we talked about this, Mum? Cass sitting here having supper, just like this."

Helen shook her head. "I don't know," she said. "Hundreds."

I cut a piece off a meatball dripping in sauce. I tried to make my face right. I tried to smile and not grimace, tried to close my eyes in delight, not panic; tried to swallow, not gag. They watched me like hawks.

"Delicious," I said, still chewing. They tasted like salt and shit and gristle.

"As good as you remember?"

"Better."

I got through two. I drank a lot of water. I broke them down into fractions of themselves, sixteen more to go, fourteen more, eight, one. In my head I said sorry to Grandad, and to the lamb or the pig or the mixture of creatures I was eating. I put my knife and fork together with four of them still swimming on my plate.

"What's wrong?" said Helen.

"That's not like you," said Edie.

I said, "I haven't eaten like this in a while. My stomach isn't quite up to it."

I allowed Cassiel, wherever he was, to chalk up a point against me. I told myself it didn't matter. I reminded myself I didn't have a choice.

So I wasn't a vegetarian anymore. I wasn't me anymore either.

When you're running, when you're moving from place to place, day after day, it's hard to watch yourself eat. You steal. You pick through the bins and try not to realize it's you. You try not to think about what you're doing. You learn where the shops dump their rubbish, what night's the best night. You rely on what other people waste.

Finish your food? No, don't, because somebody watching from outside might want it.

After meatballs there was ice cream. I let it melt in my mouth, and it slipped, rich and oversweet, down my throat. I did it without thinking.

"Why d'you always eat it like that?" Edie said. "It's gross."

Funny to have such a thing in common with Cassiel—the way we ate ice cream.

"Have you been in London? Or Bristol? Or Manchester? Or where?" Edie said.

"He's tired," Helen said, putting her cool hand on my forehead.

"Have you been living rough?" Edie said. "On the streets?"

What would the answer to that be? It was pretty likely. If you run away from home when you're fourteen, you don't usually end up in the penthouse suite.

"Now and then," I said.

Helen shook her head. "And being on the streets was better than being here?" She looked at Edie and then at me. "I don't understand."

"Nor do I," Edie said, "when you put it like that."

My stomach was giddy with rich and strange food. I listened to their spoon scrapes, their soft slurps and swallows.

"Why did you go off?" Edie said.

I looked at her food, only at her food. I said, "I didn't know what else to do."

"I don't believe you," Edie said.

I kept my voice soft. I kept it level. "You don't have to."

"What was so awful?" Helen said. "What was so bad that you had to go?"

I didn't say anything.

Edie said, "You shouldn't have punished us all like that."

"Frank said you were in trouble," Helen said. "He was worried about you."

"I don't understand why you didn't call," Edie said. "I'll never understand why you let us all think you were dead."

Was it okay to say sorry? Would Cassiel say sorry for that? I wanted to say it.

Edie couldn't stop. "You didn't think about what it would do to us," she said. "It didn't cross your mind."

"You don't know that," Helen said.

"Yes I do, Mum. I know him better than you. I'm right, aren't I, Cassiel?"

"I don't know," I said.

"I am," she said. "And you *do* know. And I will *never* forgive you."

"You said on the missing-persons thing that you'd never give up," I told her. "You didn't say you'd never forgive."

I worried instantly that I shouldn't have spoken. In the silence that followed, I thought I'd done something wrong.

"You didn't make it easy," Edie said.

Helen started to clear the plates. I got up to help her.

"Sit down," I said, my hand on her shoulder. "I'll do this."

"Nice try," Edie said. "Walk out for a couple of years and then tiptoe back in, all soft and sweet and helpful, like that's going to fool anybody."

I stacked the bowls as quietly as I could.

"Who the hell are you pretending to be, Cassiel Roadnight?" she said.

"Leave him," Helen said. "That's enough."

"I'm sorry, Edie," I said. "I'm sorry, Mum."

Edie growled.

Helen looked at me, and I smiled. "Your eyes have changed color," she said. She was surprised to hear herself say it.

I didn't move. Edie pushed the ice cream away from her and leaned toward me. "They haven't," Edie said.

"They have," said Helen. "They're different. How's that possible?"

Because I'm not him. Because I'm a grotesque copy. Because I'm a cuckoo in the nest.

"It's not possible," said Edie. "That's the point."

"Look at me," Helen said.

I didn't want to. I didn't want her to see me. "I am."

"Your eyes used to be blue," she said.

"They *are* blue."

"They've changed," Helen said. "They're not the same blue. They're darker."

I waited for them both to notice. I waited for the horror to dawn on their faces. I knew his mother would see.

"Yeah, right," Edie said under her breath. "And you can count how many fingers I'm holding up."

"What?" Helen said.

"You're not remembering them right," Edie said. "That's all it is."

"I am," Helen said. "I know my son's eyes."

Tears welled up suddenly in hers. I hated to see his mother so ruined and so upset and so completely right. It hurt. And it was my fault.

"Do you think I don't know my own son?" she said, to neither of us.

I put my arms around her. I said, "It's okay, Mum," even though it wasn't, even though if she knew the truth she would scream the house down when I tried to touch her.

"I've got to go to bed," she said. "I'm suddenly so tired."

Edie said, "Tranquilizers will do that."

"Don't, Edie," I said, without thinking.

It stunned her. It stopped her dead. I knew what the look on her face meant. I knew what she was thinking. Cassiel wouldn't have said that.

Helen took my hand and looked at it like she'd never seen it before. She kept hold of it until I moved away, until she had to let go.

She kissed me on the cheek, delicate and cool.

"'Night, Cassiel. 'Night, Edie," she said, when she was halfway up the stairs. "Sleep well."

I tried to look everywhere but at Edie. I cleared off and wiped the table and made a big deal of finding out where everything went and putting it away.

She watched me the whole time. I could feel her watching. I watched myself through her. I became aware of every little movement, every little sound, like the next thing I did would give me away.

When I'd finished, I didn't know what to do. I sat back down.

"You're not fooling me," she said.

She knows, I thought. This is over already. I made my face as blank as I could. I tried not to show her everything on it. I carried on pretending. "I'm not trying to," I said.

"I haven't forgotten what you're really like," she said. "It'd take more than two years to forget that."

"So tell me what I'm like," I said. "Maybe it's me who's forgotten."

Edie listed on her fingers, bluntly, like an ax falling. I didn't expect it. I didn't expect her sudden anger.

"Selfish," she said. "Rude. Arrogant. Unhelpful. Bad-tempered. Aggressive. Secretive. Greedy." She stopped. "How many's that?"

"It's enough," I told her. "I can see you really missed me."

She said, "I'm just wondering how long it's going to last."

Me too. That's what *I* was wondering.

"As long as I can keep doing it," I said.

She smiled. The rigid set of her face and shoulders relaxed a little. "I quite like it," she said. "If I'm honest."

"Quite like what?"

"New, improved, supernice Cassiel," she said. "Kind to his mother, helpful in the kitchen."

"Oh," I said.

"You're going to offer to take the dog out in a minute."

I looked at Sergeant. I clicked my fingers and opened the door. He got up slowly, eased himself to standing.

"God, you bloody are," she said.

I smiled at her, kept my breathing even, kept my voice calm. "I haven't done it for two years," I said. "I thought it might be my turn."

Outside, the wind had dropped, and it was black, thick with stars. I heaved in lungfuls of the cold, wet air. I breathed like I'd been underwater too long. Sergeant sniffed around in the grass, caught the scent of something, followed it off.

My first night as Cassiel Roadnight. My first day. I'd almost survived it.

The dog followed the scent straight back inside. It was the scent of his basket probably. Edie came to the door. Some of the anger had gone out of her. She smiled.

"Come in, little brother," she said. "It's freezing out there."

I did what I was told. I thought it was best.

We turned the lights off in the kitchen and closed all the doors. We tried to be quiet on the stairs.

"Good night, Edie," I said, when I got to Cassiel's door.

"'Night," she said.

I almost had it shut. I was almost alone. I'd almost done it. I had this sensation of holding my breath for the longest time, of being about to exhale.

"Cass?" she said.

"What?"

I couldn't see her face. It was too dark.

"I'm glad you're home," she said.

"Thanks."

"Even if you are being weird."

NINE

couldn't sleep. I'd never been more awake in my life. I sat on Cassiel Roadnight's bed, on my bed, like I'd sat on the bed in that hostel the night before, waiting for Edie to come. I sat completely still, but my mind would not stop moving.

This was what I had wanted. A place to call mine again, a room of my own. A family, a mum and a sister who knew me and loved me and were right there, next door, across the hall. A brother, on his way to welcome me home.

I heard Edie turning the pages of a book, heard the flick of her light going out. I heard the sigh of Helen's sheets as she turned over in bed.

Poor Helen, so broken and feeble. Had I done this to her? Had Cassiel? And Edie, who looked as delicate as her mother but was made of something different, something I could already see inside, something more like steel.

I was afraid of breaking them. And just as scared of them breaking me.

It was quiet outside. The wind had gone and the lack of sound was something thick and real, a silence I wasn't sure I'd ever heard before. There's always noise in the city at night. It's rarely quiet and it's always light. You get used to it, sleeping in the never-dark, sleeping while a plastic bag crackles like a flag in the branches of a tree above you, while trucks sigh and judder, while voices rise and fall and glasses smash and sirens rush to someone else's tragedy, somewhere else. The noise and the light are like blankets that protect you from the silence and the black.

There were no blankets here. I turned off Cassiel's light for a minute and plunged myself into total dark. I tried to hear something in all that quiet. I lost my bearings. It was like disappearing. It was absolute nothing, the lip of a bottomless void. At last, somewhere on the hill, I heard the bleat of a sheep. I was grateful to it in that moment, for reminding me that I was still here.

I put on the light, as low as it would go, and looked around. There had to be clues in here. There had to be secrets. I started to take Cassiel's room apart, drawer by drawer, page by page, inch by inch, soundlessly, looking for the real him, looking for the little things I needed to know and do and say, looking for who to be in the morning when the others woke up, when Frank came home. I crept like a burglar in my brand-new room.

I didn't find much. I didn't find nearly enough.

Cassiel's laptop was empty. It was wiped clean. His drawers were full of socks and pants and T-shirts, all too folded, all too small. There was nothing written in his books, nothing hidden in his wardrobe.

A jacket on a hanger held one piece of letter-size paper, folded three times. There was nothing written on it.

Hardly a hoard, hardly the ripe and helpless harvest my plague of locusts had been expecting. Cassiel's room was like a stage set. It was unnatural. Edie had tried to re-create it when they moved. She'd made something that looked like his room from the outside, but there was nothing of him in it, nothing of him left. She'd made a fake. She'd made something like me.

Is that what would happen? They'd search me for traces of him and find nothing? They'd take me apart and see that I was empty?

What had they done with all of Cassiel's stuff? Fourteen-year-old boys didn't have rooms this empty. They had crap and junk and clutter. They had a thousand pieces of screwed-up paper with things drawn on them, things written. They had key chains and notebooks and harmonicas and chewing gum and deodorant and binoculars and music. They had secrets, for God's sake. Where were Cassiel's secrets?

I gave up at two in the morning. I turned the light off and

sat on his bed in the dark, waiting for the numbers on the clock to change, watching the seconds flash by.

What would I do tomorrow? Keep it all locked in. Stay quiet. Tread carefully along the blade, one foot in front of the other.

How long would it be before they saw me?

Three knocks on the door snapped the silence into three loud pieces.

"Who is it?" I said.

There was no answer, but the handle turned. The door opened. It was darker out there than it was in here. I hadn't thought that was possible.

"Hello?"

It was Helen. She came in like a quiet ghost, in pale pajamas and a crumpled white robe. Her face was gaunt in the gray dark, all hollows and shadows.

"I can't sleep," she said.

"Me neither."

"I can never sleep."

Her eyes glinted. What light there was stuck to the whites of her eyes and her white clothes. She looked at me strangely, like you'd look at a person who didn't know you were watching. She drank me in.

"Do you want something?" she said. "A hot drink?"

"No," I said. "I'm fine."

To be on my own, that's what I wanted. To be off guard.

I should have gotten into bed. I should have pretended to be asleep.

She had something in her arms. "I've been looking at these," she said, and she passed me a pile of books, heavy and thick, sliding across each other as I tried to hold on to them.

"What are they?"

I turned the light on. We both put our hands up to shield our eyes.

Photo albums.

"My God," I said. "Thank you."

She stood by the bed, timid, shifting. "Can I sit down?" she said.

"'Course."

"You might not want to look at them," she said.

"No," I said. "I do."

We sat on the end of the bed without saying anything, without looking at each other. I held the books on my lap. There were eight of them. I felt their spines and edges with my fingers.

Helen put her hand on mine. "Thank you," she said.

"For what?"

"I knew you'd come back."

"Oh," I said. Just, "Oh."

I didn't look at her. I looked into the dark landing. I wondered if Edie was asleep or if she was lying awake, listening, watching the light from my room draw around her door. I didn't want her to be awake. I didn't want her to come in here as well and start talking.

Helen saw where I was looking. "She's angry with you," she said. "She's got the strength for it."

"I know."

"She'll get over it."

"Maybe."

As long as she doesn't find out.

She looked at her hands. She held them out straight in front of her, fingers outstretched. She frowned. "I think I want to forget it," she said. "I don't think I ever want to talk about it again."

"Good," I said. "Then we won't."

"Yes, we will," she said. "You know we will."

When Helen left the room I took off my jeans and sat up in bed with the books. Each one was carefully labeled with names and dates and places. I put them in order of time.

There weren't any baby pictures. The first book started when he was about three.

A little boy with fat knees and sturdy shoes. A little boy with his thumb in his mouth, and big questioning eyes. A little boy clutching a blanket.

It was the scrap I'd sat on in Edie's car. Bigger, cleaner, white and not gray, not yet. In the picture I had it tucked under my arm, wrapped around my hand. I recognized its whorls and swirls. I got it out of my bag and put it next to me, on my pillow. Cassiel's blanket.

I went through the whole eight books. I looked and learned, grabbing hold of each image, turning every little caption into memory, into armor. And when I had finished, I started with the first book again.

I fell asleep some time after four. I felt the books slide off the bed, but I couldn't wake up enough to care, to hear them land.

TEN

In the morning, when I opened my eyes in his room, heard the birds arguing and the clanking sounds of the house warming up, I knew where I was. I knew it instantly, like I was meant to be there.

I went straight to the window, to the incredible, changeable view, the shadows of clouds rolling over grassland, the shifting colors of the mountains, the blue-gray bowl of the sky. I could have stayed there all day, just watching it. I didn't want to do anything else.

I listened to Edie and Helen waking up, little scuffles and stretches, like rats behind a wall, like mice in their cages.

I wanted to keep away from them. I wanted to stay in bed so they'd know that Cassiel was asleep upstairs, so they could be happy and I wouldn't have to come out and ruin it by being me.

At about eleven, Edie opened my door. I was still in bed. "'Morning," she said.

"Yes."

She was pale and string-bean thin. She blew her hair out of her eyes, and it moved above her as if it had a life of its own.

"Sorry," she said.

"What for?"

"I'd planned not to be all angry and weird."

"It's okay," I said.

"Did you sleep well?"

"Yes," I said.

"Liar," she said, looking at the vague disorder of the room, the sprawled photo albums.

She came in and let the door bang shut. I didn't want her in here, and I didn't want her to go either. I was terrified of making a mistake. I pulled the sheet up over my chest. I propped myself on one elbow. Edie picked up an album open to pages of a long-gone Christmas.

"I was awake for ages," I said.

"Did Mum give you these?"

I nodded, yawned, rubbed at my eyes. I didn't have a toothbrush. I wanted a bath.

"She spends hours looking at these things," she said.

"I did last night," I said. "They're good. They're lovely."

She frowned at me. "See? You've changed. You've been saying the strangest things. They're *lovely*?"

"Sorry."

"Again," she said, but she was smiling. She turned the pages

72

slowly, settled herself on the floor next to the bed. I could see her profile, down to the top of her mouth. That's all I could see.

"Oh God," she said. "Do you remember that guy?"

"Hans," I said. I read the caption, that's all.

"The Dutch lodger that Mum took pity on."

"Yes. Nice shirt."

She laughed. "Do you remember that hideous windmill he gave us? With the music and the flashing lights?"

"What did it play?" I said.

"'Waltzing Matilda'? No, can't be, I don't remember."

"'A Mouse Lived in a Windmill,'" I said.

It was just a guess.

"Yes! That was it. Was it?"

She turned a few more pages. I heard the slick of them coming unstuck from one another. I shut my eyes.

"Are you getting up anytime soon?" she said.

"I don't know."

"What are you afraid of," she said. "Daylight?"

No. I'm afraid of you. I'm afraid of myself, of whatever it is I'm going to do or say to make it all go wrong. I'm desperately trying to avoid that moment and walking straight toward it, all at the same time.

"I'm just tired," I said.

She got up. She poked me in the side. She touched my cheek with her fingers, and I tried not to pull away. I tried not to lean into her either, not to put the whole weight of my head in her hand.

She drew along the line of my scar with one finger. She traced the dog bite from my cheekbone to my ear.

"How did you get that?" she said.

"I don't know."

"I don't remember you getting it," she said. "I don't remember it being there."

I wanted to put my hand out and push hers away. "Well, it is," I said.

"Maybe there's photographic evidence," she said, picking up each album in turn, scanning the dates. "Maybe if we just get the right book, we can find out."

I got up, took the albums away from her, stacked them neatly on the desk. I felt self-conscious, standing there in just my underwear. I didn't want her to see me, see the ways I might be different from her brother.

Edie watched my face. "And who punched you?" she said. "Who hit you right there, under your eye?"

"That," I said, "was just some thug."

"Why'd he hit you?" She reached up to touch the mark his diamond had made. I moved away from her hand.

"Because I can be really annoying sometimes."

Edie rubbed her cold hand against my arm. "Mmmm," she said. "My sympathies are with him."

"Get off," I said. "Stop wiping your hands on me."

She flinched when I said it. She stepped back, fast and defensive, and it occurred to me for the first time that she was scared of him. I wondered if Cassiel had ever hit her.

She went to the desk and picked up another album, a more recent one, from the year before Cassiel disappeared.

"Did you have a lot of fights out there?" she said. "Did you annoy a lot of people?"

For a second I saw myself being restrained. I felt the weight of an adult male's body against my knees, cutting off the circulation in my legs. I felt the yank of my arms, high behind my back. I heard the rasping, adrenaline-rich voice, telling me over and over again to calm down, to breathe right, to stop screaming. I felt my own helpless, ten-, eleven-, twelve-year-old's rage. I swallowed.

"I pissed a few people off," I said.

Edie opened another album to show me. I looked at her and Cassiel standing on a hill somewhere, dressed up, warm and bright against the snow.

"I did miss you," she said. "God knows why."

I didn't want her to be so nice. I didn't want her to be so tender and funny and full of love and hurt and broken trust. It was too early in the morning. I couldn't think why I was here, doing this to her. Why was I doing this?

She held up a finger. "I didn't miss you lying or shouting or stealing or sneaking around. I didn't miss you being stupid and arrogant and pigheaded and cruel. I didn't miss your crap music or your total obsession with the remote control," she said. "But I did miss you."

"Thanks," I said. "That's nice."

"I know."

She blew me a kiss and got up. "Do you want pancakes? I'm in the mood for cooking again."

"Are you in the mood for eating?" I said. "You're like a stick."

"Ha-ha," she said. "Very original. Pancakes?"

"Pancakes and orange juice and sunshine and bad jokes," I said.

"What?"

"Nothing," I said. "It's what I thought of when I thought about home."

"You thought about home?" she said.

"Of course I did. All the time."

"Well, I don't know where you got that idea from," she said, out the door by then, closing it on her smile.

I got out of bed when I smelled the pancakes. Pancakes and cigarette smoke. I could hear Helen's voice, the soft rhythm of it carrying from downstairs. I went into the bathroom and splashed my face. I used somebody else's toothbrush. I leaned on the sink, put my face close to the mirror. My hair needed cutting. I could do with a shave. The shadows around my eyes were dark and swollen. I looked.

Did I look anything like that might this morning? All I could see when I looked or was me.

Would Helen take one and know, in the cold light of day?

Would it be Frank who'd see right through me, as soon as he got here?

Was today the day it ended? Was it soon? Was it now?

They both smiled when I came downstairs. They both stopped what they were doing to look at me and smile.

"'Morning," I said.

"God, look at you," said Helen.

I wiped my hands down my crumpled shirt, my filthy jeans. "All my clothes are too small."

"I'm sure they are. You're a giant." Her smile died and she turned away.

Edie said, "You need a bath."

"That would be good."

"You can wear some of Frank's clothes, can't he, Mum?" She laughed. "I'd *love* to see you in those."

She handed me a plate with six little pancakes on it, spooned some more mixture into the pan. "Here. Syrup and butter on the table."

Helen just smoked and watched me. The ashtray was full of butts already. Her mouth worked hard, trying to hold itself around her cigarette, trying not to spread and wither and cry.

"You okay?" I said, because I knew she wasn't, because I thought I should say somethi___ _nd not just ignore it.

Her voice was quie_ _____ _tful and without hope. She said, "Where's my boy_

My whole body went co___ _opped chewing and looked at her.

"What?"

The pancake in my mouth had turned to cold sponge, wet and heavy.

"Mum?" Edie said. "Get a grip, would you?"

"I lost my boy," she said, "and this . . . this man came back."

"He's still your son," Edie said. "He's still Cassiel, aren't you?"

I swallowed my food. I looked at my plate. I breathed.

No I'm not. I'm nothing to do with her, and she knows it.

"Look at the size of his hands," Helen said. "The space you take up in the room."

I felt huge and lumbering and unwelcome.

"How did you get that big?" she said. "Without me looking after you?"

"I looked after myself," I said.

"Erm, no offense"—Edie turned the pancakes over, tucked a long ribbon of hair behind her ear—"but you look like crap."

"Thanks," I said. She winked at me.

She said, "You'll get used to him, Mum."

"I don't want to get used to him," Helen said, "I want to

be amazed and grateful every minute that he came back." She smiled at me, stubbed her cigarette ~ .said . the others. "If I get used to you again, somebody sl ...

I looked at the remains o breakfast. *Please get used to me. Please all of you get used to m nd the real Cassiel never come home, and just let me be here. Ju et me have this.*

Edie sat down and smiled at me and made a little tower of pancakes on her plate, smothered in syrup. She speared them with her fork, looked out the window, the gray and green of the garden reflected in the blue and black and white of her eyes.

Helen said she was going upstairs to make up Frank's bed.

"When's he coming?" I said.

"Soon," she said, drifting to the edge of the room, moving through the door and into the hallway and out of sight. "Later."

I looked at Edie. "She's all over the place," I said.

"She always has been."

"Really?"

"You've just forgotten. She's been worse."

"Was it me? Did I make her worse?"

"Don't flatter yourself. She was as bad when you were here as when you weren't."

"Can't we help her?"

"I have been trying," she said, frowning at me. "It's just been me."

"What about Frank?"

"He throws money at the problem. Mum doesn't need money."

"What does she need?"

"If I knew that . . ." Edie

"I'll help," I said.

"Why do I believe you?" she said. What's wrong with me?"

"I mean it," I said. "That's why."

Edie smiled at me. "Would you take it the wrong way if I said you should go away more often?"

"Yes. Why?"

"Because you're so much nicer now."

I tried to keep the smile off my face. I blushed, for God's sake. I felt it happen. That was a compliment. That was a compliment meant for me. Edie thought I was nicer than Cassiel. Edie liked me. I allowed myself to start hoping I was safe here. I started thinking it was all going to be fine.

My smile broke open. I couldn't stop it. "Thanks," I said.

"You're welcome, freak."

Some people have no idea how lucky they are. That's what I thought when I looked at Edie. Cassiel Roadnight didn't know. He should never have left home, the ungrateful idiot.

She finished her breakfast, picked the plate up and licked it clean.

"Don't tell," she said.

"I won't if you don't."

"Deal. Let's go and find you some clothes."

ELEVEN

Frank's room was small and gloomy and cluttered. Helen had made the bed, the sheets pulled taut and smooth, the pillows plumped and pinched and standing at attention. There were three screen prints of a woman's face on the wall.

"Do you like them?" Edie said.

They were simple, the face made in six or seven clean and definite lines. Each print was the same, the same sad and faraway expression. Only the colors were different. They were beautiful.

"Yes," I said. "I do."

"I did them," Edie said, turning her back on them, walking away.

"God," I said, looking at them again, getting drawn in. "You're good."

"What do you need?" Edie said, changing the subject, opening a chest of drawers.

"Everything. I've got a sweatshirt I think. My jeans aren't worth wearing."

"You're going to have to dress up as Frank," she said. "It's not going to be pretty."

"I don't care what I look like," I said.

"Well, that's another change for the better." She handed me a pile of clothes.

"Can I have a shower?" I said.

"What are you asking me for?" she said. "This is your house. You can do what you like."

No it isn't. No I can't.

It brought me back to myself, her saying that. This wasn't my house. This wasn't my family. I knew I mustn't relax or get too comfortable or allow myself to enjoy it. Not yet. As soon as I did that, I'd say something wrong and blow the whole thing wide open. I should do my best to remember that.

"Do you want to go for a walk after?" I said, putting my face to the high little window. I wanted the open space and the cutting wind. I wanted to wear myself out with walking, to slow down my thoughts. I wanted to be with Edie. I wanted to be with my sister.

It surprised me, how much I liked her. I looked at her across the room. It was the best thing, being her brother. It made pretending to be him the worst.

"Okay," she said, smiling at me. "Yeah. I'll find you a coat and stuff."

I locked the bathroom door. I hung a towel over the mirror. I didn't want to look at myself anymore. I didn't want to be reminded that I was me and not him. If only I could take a pill and forget. How perfect that would be. If ever there was a life that needed forgetting, it was mine.

I wished I could wipe it clean, like steam off a mirror, like chalk from a board, like me from the face of the earth.

I wanted so badly to forget.

I had to wear Frank's coat as well, and his boots, and his hat. Edie laughed so hard. She bent over double, and the little coatroom rang with the sound of her.

"I love it," she said. "You look like a middle-aged banker."

"I think it suits me," I said, turning up my collar, trying to look conceited and distinguished. It made her double over again. She had to wipe the tears from her eyes.

The wind threw itself at the house when we opened the door.

"Where shall we go?" I said. "Which way?"

Edie pointed, her chin tucked into her scarf, her hat pulled down. Only her eyes were visible, screwed up against the air. "That way," she said. "Let's go and look at the river."

We started walking. The beat of our footsteps, the circle of my own breathing loud in my ears, made it easy to keep going, made it impossible to stop. The stone-still mountains away to our left were watchful, on guard, reassuringly permanent. Sheep exchanged anxious glances and scattered from our path. A buzzard circled in the air above, carried by the wind, gliding on it. I'd never been in such a free and open place—me, trapped in someone else's body, me, imprisoned by my own lie. I'd never felt freer.

I turned and walked backward to see the wide slope of fields behind us, the house hidden now over the brow of the hill. The trees around it stooped and nodded, watching us go.

If I could just forget it wasn't true, this would feel right and natural, walking here with her. But I kept remembering, and all the joy it brought me fell through the floor, tried to turn everything I looked at dark and lifeless and gray. Except for her.

Edie's coat was a cornflower blue. Her eyes watered in the cold wind, her cheeks were flushed pink.

"Will you stay?" she said.

"What?"

"When everything gets back to normal, will you stay? Have you come back for good?"

"I want to. I think so."

"What about when you and Mum start arguing again, when you and Frank get started?"

"Get started at what?"

"Oh, you know." She frowned at the view. "The usual."

I didn't know. I was thinking, What about when the real Cassiel shows up?

"Do you think I'm going to run away again?" I said.

"Yes," she said. "No. I don't know what you're going to do. You kind of brought that on yourself."

She had no idea what I'd brought. I wish I hadn't brought any of it. But I couldn't wish I hadn't come.

"What happened to your phone?" she said. "Did you throw it away or sell it or something?"

"Something," I said.

"You're going to need one," she said. "And some clothes." She laughed. "You can't go around dressed as Frank for much longer."

"I haven't got any money," I said. "I haven't got a thing."

"I'll ask Frank for some," she said.

"Okay."

"I'll ask him for some pocket money," she said, her smile tight-lipped, her eyes like stone.

We walked together without talking. I felt this urge to confess. I wanted to tell her the truth. I pictured myself doing it, down on my knees. I pictured her loathing and pain.

Lying to Edie would be so much easier if I didn't like her so much.

"Are you ready for all the attention?" she said.

"What attention?" I said.

"Nobody else knows you're back yet," she said. "But once they do . . ."

I didn't say anything.

"You know what it's like around here," she said. "Somebody cuts their hair and it's a source of fascination and debate."

I laughed.

"You're going to tear things up," she said. "I think you might cause a couple of people to actually explode."

"What shall we do?" I said. "Should we make an announcement in the paper?" I was joking.

"We could," she said. "Or we could put you in a cage with a sheet on top, and wheel you into the butter market."

"Like a freak show," I said. "Lobster Baby and the Bearded Woman and the Upside-Down Man and the Long-Lost Cassiel Roadnight."

She grinned. "We could charge."

"Yes!" I said. "Sell tickets! Then I could afford my own clothes."

"That's what it will be like, though," she said. "You're going to get gawked at. You're going to get poked and prodded and questioned. It's going to be a nightmare."

It was too much to ask, to slip quietly and unnoticed into his shoes. It was what I wanted, and I wanted far too much.

"Will you be okay?" Edie said. "Do you think you will?"

I shrugged. "I don't know till it happens," I said.

We were quiet for a minute.

"What happened to you?" she said. "Are you ever going to tell us?"

"I don't know," I said. "Not yet."

"One day," Edie said.

"Maybe," I said.

Never.

We were over the hill, looking down on to the river. I hadn't seen it before. I didn't know it was there. From up high like that you could trace its winding path through the valley. It shone flat like silver, like it was solid and still, not moving, not alive with flow and eddy and fish-leap, not black and churning beneath the bodies of swans.

"Wow," I said, because I couldn't stop myself, because it took my breath away.

"What?"

"Nothing." I kept my eyes on the mirrored water. I thought fast. "I'd forgotten how good it looks, that's all. It's just good to be home."

"Frank wanted us to move away altogether, you know," Edie was saying, loud against the wind.

"Why would he want that?"

"He almost persuaded Mum to do it."

"Where to?"

"I don't know. He had this idea we should come and live with him in London."

She looked at me for a reaction. I let her talk.

"He could persuade Mum to do anything," she said. "Sometimes I think that if he told her to jump under a train, she would."

"Why?"

"Why d'you think? She doesn't like the way he is when she says no."

"Why didn't you move, then?" I asked her.

"Because of you, *stupid*," she said, banging into me. "We stayed because of you."

I thought about what Cassiel would say to that.

"Not in the same house, though."

She looked up at me. "You mind that, don't you."

I shrugged.

"I would," she said.

What should I say to that?

"I just wish you hadn't got rid of all my stuff."

"When we started going through your room," she said, "I kept thinking you were going to come through the door and have a go at us. Even though I knew you weren't there, I kept hearing you in the hall. I kept hearing you come up the stairs."

"Find anything interesting?"

She looked so sad, smiling at me. She shook her head. "I couldn't do it," she said. "It was like admitting you were dead. I left it to Mum and Frank."

"What did they do with it all?"

"I don't know."

"They should have packed it and brought it with them," I said. "It was my junk to throw out, not theirs."

I listened to the outrage in my voice. I hated myself, I really did.

"We'd already been through it once," she said. "When we were looking for you, we had to go through your stuff to try to find out why you disappeared."

I wondered if she was about to tell me, if I was about to learn something.

"And did you find it?" I said.

"No."

We looked at each other.

"Are you going to tell me?" she said, and then she answered for me. "No."

"Sorry, Edie," I said.

"Don't be," she said, and then, "No you're not."

We turned back when the wind got so cold that Edie couldn't feel her hands anymore, even with gloves. The house was quiet. Helen had gone back to bed.

"Cigarettes and sleeping pills for breakfast," Edie said. "Home sweet home."

"I wish she'd stop now," I said.

"Are you kidding? You think your coming back's going to change the habit of a lifetime? I thought you were joking yesterday," she said. "Have you really forgotten?"

I listened to the warming hum of the stove, the creak of Sergeant's basket as he circled to change position, too old to have come on a walk with us, too old and tired.

Neither of us knew what to do next.

"Let's get in the car," Edie said. "Let's go into town right now, get it over with."

"The freak show?" I said.

"Let's do it."

I didn't want to go there. I didn't want to be seen and prodded and questioned. There were so many reasons to say no.

I tried to. I said we should leave it for a while. I said, "Maybe Helen wants to come with us." I said, "Do you think we should wait for Frank?"

"Why does *everything* have to be decided by him?" Edie said suddenly. "Can we move without Frank's permission? Can we *breathe*?"

"Easy," I said. "Calm down."

"What?" she said. "Ever since you left it's like he's become the Master of the Universe or something, and we little women just don't know how to cope."

"Sorry," I said. "I didn't mean to hit a nerve."

"Talking about Frank always hits the nerve," she said. "You know what he's like."

I said, "I guess so," because I couldn't think of anything else.

"Let's just go," Edie said. "Let's decide to do something without anyone else giving us the benefit of their opinion."

What choice did I have? I couldn't say no.

"Let's go into town and scare people," she said.

"What with?"

"With *you*," she said, getting into the car, smiling at me before shutting her door. "You're the walking dead."

So we did. Against my better judgment, against all the warning noises in my head, we got into the car and Edie drove the ten minutes into town. We parked in the market square. It was almost deserted. There were two old women talking on the corner, a dog wandering around, somebody at the cash machine.

I was relieved, but I pretended not to be. "Not much of an audience," I said.

It didn't take long. The lady in the newsstand called me Frank, and Edie said, "It's not Frank. He's dressed as Frank, but he isn't him."

The lady looked again. "I don't believe it," she said. "Cassiel Roadnight. Is that you?"

Edie took my hand and pulled me toward the door. "He's back," she said, "and you are the first to know."

"How are you?" the lady said.

"I'm fine, thanks," I said, halfway out already.

"That should do it," Edie said. "Everybody goes in there. Where else? Want a coffee?"

I shrugged. "Not really."

"Well, it's not about the coffee," she said, leading the way. "It's about sitting in the window and getting seen. Let's count the double takes on people's faces."

We did. There were thirty-seven. Some of them came in and spoke straight to me, the bell on the door announcing their arrival, heralding their decision to come in. I had to smile and pretend I knew who they were without actually using their names.

"It's you," they said, and, "You're back," and I said, "Hello," and, "Yes."

Everything else, all the questions they wanted to ask, all the information they craved, went on behind their eyes. I watched it. And I didn't have to join in.

Nobody was scared. Nobody exploded. Maybe they wanted to. It must have been something, seeing a boy they probably thought was dead, sitting with his sister drinking coffee, like nothing had happened.

I thought it was going quite well, but Edie seemed disappointed.

"Where is everyone?" she said. "What time is it?"

"Twelve thirty."

"We should have come in later," she said. "If I'd thought about it, we could have come in after school, when all your mates are about. I bet you're dying to see them."

I wasn't. I was happy with just her. Mates had never been my strong point. Groups of kids were never my thing. Suddenly I felt very unsafe. I was walking on a tightrope, losing my balance. I felt the ground sway beneath me.

I couldn't see people that knew him like that, not yet. I

wouldn't know how to act around them. I didn't know how you behaved with friends. I wanted to be back in the cottage, tucked beside the hill, hidden. I stood up. My coffee cup rattled in its saucer when I moved. My chair squawked against the polished floor.

"Can we go now?" I said.

"Don't you want to hang around?"

"No."

Edie looked up at me in surprise. I was abrupt and rude. Maybe I was being more like the real Cassiel. I remember that's what I thought.

I felt sure that something bad was going to happen if we didn't leave. I put Frank's hat on. I pulled it down over my eyes.

"Why don't you want to see them?" she said.

"I do," I said. "But not now. I'm bored."

"I suppose a two-hour wait in this place might've killed us," she said.

It wasn't the waiting I was worried about.

"Let's go. Come on."

"All right, all right," she said.

I left the café before Edie did. The bell on the door rang once when I opened it and once when it closed behind me while she was paying the bill. I got to the car before her. I got in.

"You still hate it here, then," Edie said, catching up and getting in without looking at me, putting the key in the ignition.

"Yep," I said.

The engine started. In the passenger-side mirror I could see part of a castle that towered over the parking lot. I wondered when its now-ruined battlements and crumbling walls guarded something other than a parking meter, something more than a collection of old books.

Edie said, "One day I'll get out too."

"Where?" I said while she backed slowly out of the parking space, turned the car into the road.

"Maybe next year I'll go to college."

"What would you do?"

"Art, I guess. You knew that."

"'Course. Sorry."

"Most of my friends have gone," she said. "They come back at Christmas, and maybe a couple times a year." She smiled. "Trailing life behind them."

"Why aren't you at college already, then?" I said.

"I didn't want to go."

"Why not?"

"I told you. I wanted to be here when you got back."

So it was Cassiel's fault.

"Sorry," I said, for him.

"Don't be."

But I was.

I wondered how long she would have waited. I wondered if she would have stayed here forever, putting herself on hold, waiting for Cassiel. Was he ever planning to come back? Did he know that when he left? Did he think about it? Did he care?

Edie waved at a woman with a baby, a balding man, at an old lady with a shopping bag.

"That'll do it," she said, nodding at the old lady. "If you only told her, everyone would know you were back by tomorrow."

I didn't want that. The more people that knew, the more likely I was to slip up and get caught out.

It was a mistake to have come into town with her. It was stupid, showing off like that. It was careless. I'd just wanted to be with Edie. And being with Edie was making me incautious, was going to get me noticed.

I didn't want to get caught out. I didn't want to leave like she did. I didn't hate it at all.

I looked at Edie. I watched her and she didn't know it. Maybe now that I was here she'd do something more than just waiting. Maybe she would go to college. Now that I was back, she could go.

Maybe she'd leave me, just when I'd found her.

I wanted to know how long I could be her brother. I wanted to know if I could do it forever.

"The freak show is leaving town," she said, and I waved with her, even though I didn't know who any of them were, just to do the same thing she did.

TWELVE

When we got back to the house, Frank's car was there. I didn't need anyone to tell me it was his. The license plate said FR4NK. I felt the ball of tension grow in my chest, rise up in my throat, pull and tighten all the muscles in my body.

"Stuck-up jerk," Edie said, grinning at me, bringing her grubby silver Peugeot to a stop next to his gleaming, monstrous 4x4, a little too close for him to open his own door.

"Accident," she said, shrugging. "What can I say? Woman driver."

The front door of the house was locked. She banged on it three times, hard. "He locks everything," she said. "He's obsessive."

I didn't say anything. I shut my eyes. I swallowed. I could hear my heart beating in my ears. I could feel it shake me.

What if he knew I was me? What if he looked at me and just said, "No"?

Edie opened the letterbox, put her mouth to the gap. "Frank!"

"There's no hurry, is there?" I said.

"It's freezing out here," she said. "I don't like being locked out of my own house."

I heard him coming down the stairs. I pictured him coming through the kitchen to the door. I felt him just on the other side, taking up all the space, ready to condemn me.

"Let's get a look at him," he said, turning the lock, switching the bolt. "Is he there? Cass! Are you there?"

"Yes." My voice sounded lost and far away.

The door opened and he stood there, dark like Cassiel and sharper, more handsome, his hair short and neat, his face healthy and tanned. I saw money when I looked at Frank. I saw wealth and comfort and things I'd never dared to start wanting. He put one hand up in a still wave and stared. I did the same.

There was a strange lull while nothing happened. I counted to three in my head as he looked at me and I looked back, and I tried to be ready for whatever happened next. At first, Frank's eyes seemed dark and unsmiling. I got the sensation of something lurking there, of something leaving, but not before I'd glimpsed it out of the corner of my eye.

I felt it in my bones, the fear that he could see I wasn't Cassiel.

Edie hung back.

I waited.

The strong lines of Frank's face lifted into a smile, the smile cracked into a laugh. His teeth were white and straight and even. His mouth danced. He held his hands out to me. I was in.

"Cass," he said. "Little brother."

Relief coursed through me, a sudden warmth in my veins. I smiled back, my own cracked and crooked smile meeting his perfect one.

"Hello, Frank," I said.

He shook my hand, clapped me on the back, hugged me. "Let me look at you," he said. "Not so little anymore. God."

He was taller than me. He held me by the shoulders and studied my face, every inch of it. He took my chin in his right hand and moved my face from side to side. For a moment I felt like a painting of Cassiel, a sculpture, like I was a thing and Frank was buying me.

He put his arms around me and held on tight, his voice rich and warm in my ear. "Very good," was all I heard. I didn't hear him right.

"What?"

"Have you any idea how good it is to see you?"

I tried to nod. He was holding on to me so hard, I couldn't move.

I tried to say, "I think so," but my mouth just came up against the wool of his sweater, coarse and perfumed and hot.

He kissed me once on the side of the face, a kiss loud with joy and relief. "Where did you come from?" he said.

I shrugged. It was all I could do.

"I don't care," he said. "I don't need to know. Let's go in."

He put his arm around my shoulders, drew me across the kitchen. Edie followed us in and shut the door. Helen stood in the corner, her hands clasped together. Frank's skin was smooth and poreless, clean-shaven. His smile was like a light, making safe the dark corners of the room. I couldn't take my eyes off him. My new big brother.

It wasn't like meeting Edie. It wasn't like having a sister I wanted to look after. With Frank, I felt like someone was going to look after me. I hadn't felt like that in way too long. I was almost weak with the relief of it.

He held me again at arm's length and looked at me. "Where have you been?" he said. "Has anyone asked you that yet? Where the hell have you been?"

I didn't answer.

He said, "Where'd you pick up those scars?"

I felt myself flush. I knew the dog bite would show up pale against my reddening skin; I knew the diamond cut would get darker. Would the marks from a dog and a boy called Rigg give me away?

"I'm all right," I said. "They're nothing."

He looked me in the eyes and then away and around the room. "He's really back," he said to Helen and Edie, as if saying it out loud made it true. It felt like that to me. "He's really here."

He turned to me again then, his light fell on me. "Back from the dead," he said. "Our own Lazarus."

"Oh!" Helen said, clutching her cardigan about her. "Don't say that."

"Where's the champagne?" Frank said. "Did I leave it in the car?"

He went out, left the front door open, his city clothes instantly wind-flattened against his frame.

"You okay, Mum?" Edie said.

"Of course." Helen smiled. "I couldn't be better." The sound of her was all joy, but her eyes were hardly there, I could see that.

"I'll make some coffee," Edie said.

"No, champagne!" Frank said, striding back in, pushing the door shut with his foot. "Get some glasses, Edie."

"I don't think Mum needs one." Edie's voice was low.

"You want one, don't you, Mum?" he said.

"Of course," Helen said.

Frank eased the cork out of the bottle smoothly, expertly, with a sigh instead of a pop. The champagne rushed to leave the bottle, like sea-foam. He poured four glasses, passed them out.

"A toast," he said.

"Oh yes," Helen said.

"To you," Frank said, looking me in the eyes with warmth and confidence. "To Cassiel. To all of us together again."

Edie raised her glass. "However long that lasts," she said.

Frank ignored her. "Welcome back, Cassiel," he said.

"Thanks," I said, and I meant it. I looked at him when I said it. I looked at each of them in turn, Edie and Helen and Frank. I wanted to remember this moment for as long as I could. I wanted to hold it still and keep it.

"Thank God you came back," he said.

I told the truth. "It's good to be home."

"I bet it is," he said.

The champagne tasted light and sweet and sharp and acid. Frank topped up my glass. "Do you like the new house?" he said.

I thought about everything before I said it. It needed to be just right. My mind felt lightning-quick. It danced, one step ahead. That's how it felt. I couldn't go wrong.

"It's great. A dream come true, right, Mum?"

Helen smiled and nodded, sipped her champagne.

"They found you in London, did they?" Frank said. He pulled a chair out from the table and sat down. He was the owner of this house. Everything about the way he moved and spoke in here said he was.

"Yes. In Hackney."

"Have you been in London all this time?"

Had I? Had he? "Yes," I said.

"Did you go straight there, when you left?"

"I got the train," I said. "Yes."

"Strange," he said, picking up the bottle again, pouring himself another glass.

"What is?" Edie said, so I didn't have to. I thought for a moment that I'd said something wrong, that Frank knew something different. I thought for a second that this was going to unravel.

"Strange that we've been in the same city, all this time, you and I."

"It's a big place," I said. "A lot of people are there at the same time."

He nodded, slowly, thoughtfully. "Seven million," he said, "and counting. But still, two of them were you . . ."

Frank pointed, and I thought he'd finished. I thought he knew there were two Cassiel Roadnights. I felt hot. I burned under the spotlight. Then he turned his finger on himself and said, ". . . and me."

"I like that," Helen said. "It's as if you've been together."

"Hardly," said Edie.

Frank said, "It gives you comfort, though, doesn't it? Cassiel and I have been close by all along."

"Just like old times," Edie muttered, and there was something in her voice, something bitter about the way she said it.

Frank smiled and raised his glass to me. I tried to smile back. I was rigid with the fear of being uncovered. My face didn't want to move.

"Like your room?" he said.

"My room's great."

Edie said, "He wants to know what you did with all his stuff."

Helen lit a cigarette.

"Did you lose something?" Frank said. "Are there things missing?"

"Bits and pieces," I said.

"Nothing specific?"

"It just feels a bit light in there," I said. "A bit empty."

Frank leaned back and put his feet up on the table, one ankle over the other. His shoes were black and highly polished. Expensive leather brogues. The soles were scratched and discolored from use, soft cream turned to pavement.

"We searched it, Cass," he said. "We did, and the police did. We had to. You don't mind."

"We were looking for you," Helen said.

"Did you find much?" I said. I don't know why I asked. I was being overconfident. It was reckless of me to turn the questions on him. I saw myself wading out into dark water, not knowing the way back.

"No."

"And then you moved," I said. "I suppose things get thrown out when that happens."

"Exactly."

"What about my computer?" I asked. "Did you wipe that clean? Did the police do that?"

Frank frowned. "No," he said, putting his feet back down, moving one long leg and then the other, sitting forward with his elbows on the table. "You did that, didn't you, Cass? I thought you did that."

"Oh," I said, my winning streak dropping out from underneath me. What a mistake to make. "Oh, yeah."

"We thought you did it so we couldn't find you," Frank said. "That's what the police said. Were they wrong?"

I didn't say anything.

Frank looked at Edie. "What did they say, Edie? You remember, don't you?"

Edie looked at Frank and then at me. "They said it was an indication that you had planned to leave. They said we should take it as proof that you hadn't met with an accident or something, that it was a premeditated act."

I counted to ten. It was Cassiel's turn to speak, I knew that. It was up to him to say something.

"I'm sorry," I said. "I'm sorry I let you all down."

The lights from a car swept the front of the house and went out. I hadn't realized it was starting to get dark until then. I hadn't had any idea of time passing.

"Who's that?" Edie said.

My face tightened. I was suddenly aware of the skin on my arms and my neck.

"I don't know," Helen said. "Are we expecting anybody?"

Frank got up. "No," he said, looking at me, smiling. "We're all here, remember?"

I didn't like the way he said it. I felt the edge of the tightrope I was walking. I felt the sway of the ground far below.

Edie went over to the window, put her face to the glass. She used her hands to block out the reflection of us on the inside. Frank opened the door. The light and warmth of the kitchen were so different to the blue-gray cold of outside. It was like another world out there.

I tried to think who would drive here now, to this house in the middle of nowhere. I tried not to think they'd be coming for me.

"It's two men, I think," Edie said. "I don't know who they are."

"God," I said, before I could take it back.

"What?" Helen said.

I clenched my fists. How had they found me? What traces of myself had I left behind?

"That was quick," Frank said.

I looked over at him. What did that mean? Did he know? Had he expected them to catch me?

"Who is it, Frank?" Helen said.

He didn't answer her. He left the house. He went to meet them on the porch. I felt my chest seize up, my lungs contract so I couldn't get enough air, so I was fighting to breathe.

"What's the matter, Cass?" Edie said from across the room. She looked at me. Helen and Edie both looked at me.

I didn't answer them. Everything I had was focused on the door, on who was about to come through it. Social services. The child-catcher. The police.

I held my breath, and when Frank walked back in, he held my gaze. He smiled.

I wondered what he saw when he looked at me. He couldn't miss the terror on my face.

One of the men was young, with a big digital camera and gelled hair and a cheap suit. The second was older, gray and overweight. He wore a jacket that smelled of wax and wet dog.

"Hello," they said, a little awkward, a little shy.

The older one said they were sorry to intrude. They looked around the room, and their looking stopped at me.

My head pounded. My palms were wet. I rubbed them against my trousers. I tried to wet my lips with a dry tongue. I didn't say anything. I didn't smile, I didn't move. I waited.

Frank's eyes were on me too, but when he spoke, he spoke to us all.

"Mum, Edie, Cassiel, I hope you don't mind. These gentlemen are from the local paper."

"Oh," Helen said. She looked at Frank for approval. She looked from Edie to me and she smiled.

Both men stepped toward her to shake hands. "We phoned earlier," the younger one said. "We spoke to . . . erm—"

"You spoke to me," Frank said. "Sorry, everyone. I forgot to mention it."

He looked at me and winked. I felt the belt around my chest loosen a notch or two.

"We heard some reports today, in town," the older man said. "A few sightings. Of your son."

He looked at me when he said it. Everyone looked at me.

They hadn't come to get me. They weren't going to take me away.

Edie raised her eyebrows and smiled. "Freak show," she mouthed.

Did Helen mind, they were saying, did any of us mind if they took a picture, if they did a little piece?

Frank said, "I think it's a brilliant idea. I'm really sorry. I just forgot about it in all the excitement. You all right with it, Cass?"

"Yes," I said, just waiting for my pulse to slow down. Just hoping for the rigor mortis of pure fear to leave my face. "Yeah, sure."

The younger one walked over to me, reached out to shake my hand. "Cassiel."

"Hello," I said. Was I supposed to know him? Didn't

everybody know everybody in a town like this?

"Welcome back."

"Yeah. Thanks."

"Let's get one of all of you together."

We stood together in front of the table with our glasses raised. I half expected somebody to notice how fake it all was, to say something. I was exhausted from just being afraid all the time, from always looking over my shoulder for the enemy. I was hollowed out.

"This is great news," the older one said. "You must all be so happy."

"We are," Frank said. "We're stunned. We're over the moon."

It all went down in a notebook. Everything he said went down. I thought how funny it was, how ironic, that when something extraordinary happens, when someone tries to say how they feel and really means what they're saying, it just sounds like garbage. It sounds like words picked out of a hat. There's no way to describe those extremes of joy or sadness. *My world has fallen apart. I'm over the moon. This is the best, the worst, the saddest, the happiest day of my life.* There are no words.

The man said, "Did you ever think you'd see Cassiel again?"

"Absolutely," Frank said. "We knew he'd come back one day, didn't we, Mum? We never gave up hope."

The camera flashed and clicked and caught us, caught me. I felt wooden. My tongue was tied down, my hands were too heavy, my ears burned hot. The white-blue light made me blink, left itself on my retina, a blind square.

Frank was calm and impressive. He sounded like the Roadnight family were accepting an award.

"We want to thank everyone who has supported our campaign to get Cassiel back," he said. "We want to thank them for all their hard work and for this happy ending."

The man from the paper said, "Do you want to say something, Cassiel? Do you want to make a statement?"

I shook my head. "It's just nice to be home," I said.

Helen was flushed with drink and pills and happiness. She didn't say a word. She just smiled into the middle distance for the camera.

Edie was quiet. She took hold of my hand. "You all right?" she said.

I nodded. I couldn't speak.

"It's all a bit much for you, isn't it," she said.

"Just a bit."

"Bloody Frank. Such an actor. Anyone would think you actually *liked* each other."

It was funny, the way she said it, like a joke. I laughed at her. I laughed at all of it.

I was going to be in the paper. Cassiel was officially, publicly back. I was trying to figure out if that meant I had won, if that meant I could relax, just a little.

Except, what if he saw me?

What if, wherever he was, he saw what I had taken from him? He might know I was back already. He might not be that far away.

Frank walked the men to their car, once they had what they wanted. I watched the three of them through the window. Frank shook their hands, he clapped them on the back. He made a joke and they laughed, dutiful and self-conscious.

I looked at my hands, surprised I couldn't see through them, concerned by my own surprise. I was worn out from worrying, from being on my guard. I was stretched so thin.

"Are you staying?" Helen asked Frank when he came back in.

"Of course. For a couple of days," he said. "For as long as I can."

"That's great," she said, tipping her glass while she spoke, letting the last of the champagne slide into her open mouth. "That's wonderful."

"It's a very special occasion," Frank said. "Isn't it, Cassiel."

I smiled. "Yes, it is."

Edie touched Helen on the shoulder. "You've got both your boys home, Mum. How does it feel?"

Helen didn't say a word. She didn't look at anyone. She just nodded, the glass still to her mouth, the tears gathering in her eyes.

"It feels great," Frank said for her. "It feels like a new lease on life, doesn't it, Mum?"

Another life altogether, Frank. A double life. That's what it was.

THIRTEEN

You couldn't breathe for all the love in the Roadnight house. I couldn't breathe.

It was like trying to survive underwater. I just wasn't built for it.

I lived each day, each hour and second, under a microscope. The whole time I knew that any minute, any little thing I might say or think or do could set the alarms off, could alert them to the fact that they were drowning a total stranger in love.

Imagine getting something so precious, something you've wanted all your life, and then being so afraid of it, you can never enjoy it because you can't stop worrying it's going to break. That's how it was. I didn't know how to have this thing, this family. I didn't know how to have it and not destroy it.

I'd wanted a proper family for so long, a loving home, a place in the world like other people had. Then I got myself one. But it wasn't mine. And so far it wasn't what I thought it would be; it didn't feel like I thought it would feel.

It was like being on camera, it was like acting in a never-ending play, it was like living in a cage.

I locked myself away like a secret. I kept myself to myself. I hardly spoke at all. It seemed the best way to stay out of trouble.

We didn't go back into town. I didn't get any new clothes. I was too scared to go anywhere, too anxious to leave, because if I turned my back on any of it, it might disappear.

The others didn't seem too surprised. Maybe they thought I was adjusting. Maybe they thought that coming back after such a long absence was bound to be strange, was bound to take time. They took my reclusive, jumpy behavior in their stride like it was something they were used to. They didn't push me to get out more, or be around people. They didn't ask me why I wouldn't see any of my friends. They were very thoughtful. They were so considerate. I wondered if Cassiel had been like this when he was around. Perhaps I was doing a better impression of him than I realized. Maybe he could be moody and paranoid and fear-struck, just like me.

Only I could see the difference, hiding out in Cassiel's body. Only I could see it, trapped inside the truth, watchful and wishing I was free. I'd told this lie, and now I was responsible for keeping it, and it was like being chained down, like carrying a dead weight, like being pinned to a wall.

Sometimes a look from Helen, something Edie said, Frank's warm hand on the back of my neck, would leave me trembling with the need to tell them. For a moment I'd want to scream and thrash and kick until they were all gone, until everything was gone.

A part of me began to long for nothing the same way I used to long for a family. With the same hunger I'd had to be Cassiel, I started to wish I was nobody again. I started to wish I was separate, apart and alone, not like everybody else. Sometimes, all I wanted to do was take the lie back, not say it, never to have said it.

You can never change what's happened. I knew that.

But I started to think I could never change what's meant to happen either.

I started to think I had no control over what came next, that nothing I could do would make a difference. That no matter how well I hid it, how hard I tried, they'd find out the truth in the end.

Maybe a part of me wanted them to.

Look at me. I wanted to free myself from being me, from being Chap, the hunted, so I became Cassiel Roadnight, someone already caught and thrown in prison. Somebody battened and tethered and cornered with love.

It was suffocating. I was suffocating. Was that what was meant to happen?

I spent my days balancing on a high wire, on the air-thin blade of a knife, trying not to get noticed, trying not to let everything come tumbling down, sliced in half. And I started to think that there wasn't any point. That the truth was coming, like a bullet, ready to hit me right between the eyes.

Grandad would have warned me against it, wishing for a family, wishing for a normal life. According to him, normal was never what it looked like. He said that every family, without exception, had some dark shadow at the center of it, some terrible secret.

He said, "Otherwise, life would be too boring and we'd all give up."

I asked him what our secret was.

"Not telling," he said.

"Why not?"

"It's a secret for a reason," he told me, tapping the side of my nose with his long waxy finger.

"What's the reason?" I said.

"It's better that way."

He should have told me then. That was his chance to do it right, and he missed it.

Still, there was love in Grandad's house. It just wasn't something we had to say and display and demonstrate all day long. It wasn't something I felt trapped inside or guilty for. It was mine, I suppose. That's why, that's the difference. And it was quiet.

Grandad said he loved me only once. That was after we

weren't allowed to know each other anymore. That was when I hated him with every atom of energy I could gather. It was the saddest, most infuriating thing I ever heard.

Just because he didn't say it before, though, doesn't mean I didn't know it for a fact, like I knew that water was made of hydrogen and oxygen, like I knew that cats could climb trees.

Grandad loved me in the books he chose to read to me. In the squares of chocolate he would pull from his jacket pocket, from under the clock, from behind my own ear. In the shine on my shoes, polished like he'd been taught as a boy, with spit and elbow. In the key around my neck that meant I could go wherever I wanted and he'd always trust me to come back.

In the way he woke me up, always a gentle hand on my head, always a smell of fresh whiskey. "Chap, there's a good boy. The day's begun."

In Cassiel's room, in Cassiel's life, I woke up early every morning with one thought in my head, one word.

Stop.

I slept badly. I had angry, hunted dreams. Even the slightest noise would wake me, heart pounding, bolt upright, caught; even the sigh of leaves, even my own breathing, rapid and uneven in the dark.

My heartbeat swished in my ears all day long and drummed on my pillow at night. My hands shook when I splashed my face with water. Sometimes when I looked in the mirror I wasn't sure if I was me anymore. I was fading at the edges. I thought my mind was going. I could feel it go.

I hadn't wanted to be me. But being who you are isn't really a matter of choice. Everybody knows that.

I was Cassiel Roadnight on the surface, but inside I was the lunatic in the attic, the madman in his cell, wailing and jabbering, and scratching and battering the door down to get out.

I couldn't go on much longer. I couldn't do it anymore. I told myself it didn't matter how much I wanted this. It had to stop.

FOURTEEN

I left the house while it was still dark, before anyone else was awake. I had to dress as Frank. I looked for my old clothes, the ones I'd arrived in, but someone had thrown them away. I took a scarf and a coat off the peg, a pair of boots. I wouldn't have lasted very long in the cold without them.

I walked down the path, through the gates, and across the fields, into the open wind, the air almost sharper than I could stand. The light came up around me as I walked. The mountains appeared from behind their bed of clouds, as if they were waking up at the same time as me.

I was alone.

I walked for more than an hour before I stopped. The farther I got from the house, the more I felt like me again, whoever that was.

I thought about them sleeping in their beds, Frank and

Helen and Edie. How hard would it be for them to lose Cassiel a second time?

No harder than what I was making them do. Not if they knew.

I never used to think I was a bad person. It didn't matter how often people told me I was, I didn't believe them; I knew they were wrong. But then I stole Cassiel's life, and I wasn't so sure anymore. I made all the things they said about me come true, just like that.

I didn't see him coming because of the clouded, foggy air that clung to the tops of things, slow to lift. Objects loomed from it suddenly—rocks, trees, people. One person.

A boy. Tall and lanky and thin and wearing black.

Maybe I could have avoided him, gone wide or crouched behind a gorse bush, but at the time I thought it was too late. We appeared before each other in the thick morning. That's how I remember it. We loomed. He saw me. I heard him say Frank's name, not to me, just quietly, to himself.

I kept my head down, nodded, tried to get past. I stole a look at him.

He was my age, tall as me, dark-skinned, Indian maybe, in an old sort of tailcoat and a red scarf and a battered bowler hat. He looked like he'd just run away from the circus, with shining shaggy black hair and huge, bewildered eyes. He was bleached—no, green, like he was going to pass out or be sick. He looked stricken to see me. He looked terrified.

"Cass?" he said. His voice cracked.

I stopped, we both stopped still the moment he said it, like there was nothing else that could be done. Just my luck, to avoid all of Cassiel's friends and then run into one just when I was leaving.

He said, "You're not Frank? Are you . . . Is that Cassiel?"

I didn't want to say anything. I tried to walk on.

"It is," he said, stopping me, putting his hand on my arm. "You are. You can't be."

"Can't be what?" I said.

"You're dead," the boy said to me. "Are you dead?"

"No, I'm not."

"Why didn't I know?" He was shocked. His eyes pooled out, black and empty. He was in shock.

"What?" I said. I thought everyone would know after my visit to town. That's what Edie said.

"Why didn't you tell me?" he said.

I couldn't move away from him, from the look on his face, a look of horror and relief, a fight between them.

"Are you a ghost?" he said to me, quietly, like this was just between us, like we weren't alone.

"No. Look. You've got your hand on my arm."

He snatched it away, and then he put it back, wrapped his

hand around my bicep, checking for flesh and bone. The color in his face was coming back.

"Shit," he said. "Fuck."

He pushed the hat to the back of his head with one finger, scratched in his hair. He held his hands up in the air like someone was pointing a gun at him, a gun he found more amusing than scary. Everything he did, the way he moved, was elegant and hypnotic, like a dance. I don't think he was doing it on purpose. He just had this thing about him, this strange, graceful thing. I noticed it straight away. It wasn't something I'd normally notice.

He stared at me.

"Cassiel Roadnight," he said, one hand on his forehead, the other out toward me in a question. "Am I seeing things?"

"Yes, you are," I said.

"Am I?" he said. "Sorry. *Fuck*. Are you for real?"

"What?"

He closed his eyes, and the light went out of his face. "I'm out for a walk," he said. "Well into another boring day in my lonely miserable life, and suddenly . . ." His eyes opened again; I looked right into them. "There you are."

I waited.

"You're haunting me," he said.

"No."

"Then you're back from the dead."

"I'm not dead," I said. "I wasn't dead."

He laughed. "I must've got it wrong, then."

"Yes," I said. "You must have."

"I'm glad," he said, and then he groaned and looked at the ground, like he was the opposite of glad; put the heels of his hands on his eyes, pressed hard.

"I've got to go," I said.

"That's it?" he said. *"You've got to go?"*

I asked him what he'd like me to say.

"'Hello, Floyd' would be a start."

Floyd. His name was Floyd.

"Hello, Floyd."

He grabbed me and hugged me, and as quickly as he'd done it, he let go. "Sorry," he said.

"That's all right."

He looked into the sky. He raised his hands, palms up, like he was Jesus, like he was asking God a question. Then he pointed at me, like he was asking it about me.

"What's going on?" he said.

"I don't know," I said.

"What happened?"

"I don't want to talk about it," I said. "Not right now."

"Oh," he said. "Oh, right. Okay."

I smiled at him, but he didn't smile back. I didn't know what he was talking about. I didn't know what to say. I just wanted to keep moving.

He said, "How about now?"

"What?"

"Now? Any good?"

"No," I said.

"Well, when *do* you want to talk about it, Cassiel?" Floyd said. It burst out of him like a gunshot—caustic, sarcastic.

"I don't," I said. "I don't want to."

"That's not really working for me," he said.

"I'm sorry," I said.

"What for?" he said. "For which bit of it?"

"What do you mean?"

"If I'm not back in three hours," he said, *"take this stuff and use it. Hide it. Keep it safe. I'm dead."*

He was quoting me. He was quoting Cassiel. It took a second for me to work that out.

"What?" I said.

"Forget it," he said.

"Hold on," I said. "Go back." But he wouldn't.

"And now, I bump into you, taking a stroll like nothing's happened, and you say you don't want to talk about it?"

Floyd put his hand on my chest, put his face right up to mine. His eyes were black with fury. "What's going on?" he said.

"What? Wait a minute," I said.

I went over what he'd said. I tried to listen to it again in my head, but Floyd was still talking. He was shouting at me.

"Are you going to pretend I'm not here? Is that how it's

going to be? Is it going to be like that again?"

"I don't know."

"Do you know anything?" he said. "Are you going to say *anything* that counts?"

I started shaking. I could feel this tremor move through me, and I couldn't make it stop. It had nothing to do with willpower, nothing do with what I thought. It was my body rebelling against my mind. It was me cracking up. That's what it felt like. I shook, and I looked at Floyd to see if he'd notice.

"Are you okay?" he said.

"Not really."

"What's going on?"

"I have no idea," I said. "I really don't."

"Shit, Cassiel. Are you still in trouble?"

I nodded. More than you could know, I thought.

"What's going on?"

"I was thinking about running away again," I said.

"Very funny."

"I'm not joking."

"You're not dead."

"I guess not."

"Well, it's a start." He grinned. "Never been happier to be wrong about something in my whole life."

"Good," I said. "Thanks."

He looked at me funny. He frowned at me and looked away.

"Where have you been?" he said.

"Went to London."

"Didn't think to let anyone know? Was I a smoke screen? Was that it?"

"No, I don't think so."

"What was I, then?"

"I can't tell you."

"I can't give you your stuff back."

I didn't ask him what stuff. I said, "Why not?"

"I don't have it."

"I'm confused," I said.

"You're not alone. Is Frank at home?"

"Yes."

"Jesus. How's that been?" Floyd said.

I shrugged.

"Have you seen everyone? Have you seen, you know, your crowd yet?"

I said I hadn't. I said I'd been spending my time with my family. I said, "I'm not ready for a crowd."

He smiled bitterly. "Not like you."

"Maybe it is now," I said.

He laughed. He thought that was funny.

"Floyd," I said.

"Yes?"

"Tell me what happened."

"You know more than I do."

"Just tell me your side," I said. "I want to hear it."

"You forgotten it?" He laughed. He started backing away, like suddenly he had to go.

"Yeah. Something like that," I said.

"Firework night," he said. "Remember? Crowds and rockets and a bonfire and a big Wicker Man and you, making up all sorts of crap about being in danger, and then disappearing. Ring any bells?"

I said, "I just want to hear it from your side."

He looked at his watch. "Okay, if you want," he said. "I'll meet you. Let me just go and do what I need to do, and I'll meet you."

"Where?"

"Clock tower."

I'd have to find it.

"You'd better be there," he said. "This better not be some weird dream or those mushrooms. Did I take those? You'd better not be them."

"Floyd," I said.

"What?"

"I'm not mushrooms."

"No," he said. "You're much worse."

"It's good to see you too," I said.

He grinned, walked backward a little more, saluted me, and then he turned.

I watched him walk away, his coattails alive behind him in the wind, his stride long and loping. He didn't look like the sort of friend I'd expected Cassiel to have, which proved how little I knew. I watched him, and then I turned around and walked back, the sky fully up now, the day fully begun.

What had Floyd been talking about? What trouble was Cassiel in? I wanted to know. I was going to stay another day to see if it changed anything.

Suddenly I wasn't leaving anymore.

FIFTEEN

Helen and Frank and Edie were sitting at the kitchen table when I got back. Helen stubbed out her cigarette. She said, "I thought you were in bed."

"I needed some air."

"How was it?" Edie said. Her hair was wet, just washed. She looked very young.

"Good," I said. "I saw Floyd."

Helen coughed suddenly and convulsively, like she'd just breathed in water. Edie went white and shook her head at me, a quick, tight, definite warning.

Only Frank didn't react. I don't think he heard. He was reading the paper, and he closed it, shook it out, and folded it neatly—rustle, crack, and rustle. He showed me the cover. There was a picture of us, dead center, under the headline HOME AT LAST. I took it out of his hand.

"'Cassiel Roadnight, of Felindre, near Hay-on-Wye, has

returned to his family after a long absence,'" I read out loud. "'Cassiel went missing at Hay on Fire two years ago, and his family have fought long and hard to find him. "This is a vindication of all our hard work," said his sister, Edie.'"

"No I didn't," Edie said. "We all know I never said a word."

"'Cassiel's brother, Frank, a banker now living in London, and his mother, Helen . . .'"

Helen pointed at herself and giggled.

"'. . . said they couldn't be more delighted and overjoyed at his safe return.'"

I studied the photo. I didn't look like an impostor. I looked real and clean and loved and at home. I looked like Cassiel Roadnight. It's amazing what storms your face can hide, what terrible wrecks can writhe and heave beneath, without one ripple on the surface. I looked at that picture and saw a family reunited with their son. It was thrilling.

But under the thrill, and the weird swell of pride, there was a black seam of panic, like coal deep under the swell of the hills around us. I let it play out in my head like a movie.

Wherever he was, Cassiel saw the picture of him that wasn't him. He snatched up the paper to take a closer look, this picture of me with his family, bunching it up in his fists. He tore out my face, a ragged square in his pocket, a space in the picture where I . . . where he had been. Cassiel Roadnight was on his way back to take everything.

I could feel him getting closer. He was on the train,

watching the country slip by, watching his face, our face, in the window. I saw him walking up the long hill to the new house. I had this sudden crystal-clear picture of him at the front door. The boy whose life I'd stolen, finally home. I had this instant crippling vision of us meeting here in this room, of us coming face-to-face, me and my lie. Frank would go out on the porch to meet him. I imagined him coming in with his arm around his real brother, the same way he had done with me. I would try to get past them, out through the door, but someone would stop me. I would throw myself through a window, all blood and glass, and flee into the night.

Frank was talking to me. I dragged myself into the room again, into reality.

"Isn't it great?" he said. "Now it's official."

"Yes," I said.

"Seeing it in print like that," Helen said, "makes it real. It really brings it home."

"Yes, it does," said Frank. "Cass is home and nobody can take him away from us."

Yes they can, I thought. And you'd never guess who.

I went to his room. I put a chair by the window and I sat, watching for him. What would happen when Cassiel Roadnight showed up at the door?

If I saw him coming, I could run. I could leave by one door, and he could enter by another, seamless, the switch unnoticed, the kindest thing. The others wouldn't have to know, then. I wouldn't exist. They wouldn't need to hate me.

That's what I was scared of, more than anything.

I didn't have to run. I could stay and fight. I could open the door to him and say, "Go away. I got here first. You are already here." Or I could wage war. I could lie in wait for him. I could sit here, at the top of my castle, on the lookout for the enemy. I could bring the fight to him. I could stop him from ever arriving.

Would I wipe Cassiel Roadnight off the face of the earth, if I had to, to protect what I had? When it came to it, would I make that choice?

I sat by the window and watched and wondered. How much did I want this? How far was I prepared to go?

Not to murder. I couldn't do that, however much I wanted what I'd taken.

Edie came in without knocking. "What are you doing in here?" she said.

"Thinking."

My hands were gripping the sides of the chair so hard that they ached. I let go and flexed my fingers. I didn't take my eyes off the window. I didn't get up.

"What's the matter?" she said. "What's wrong with you?"

"Nothing. I'm fine."

"Do you hate being home?" she said.

"Why?"

"Do you hate playing happy families?"

What was I meant to say to that? Happy families is a dream come true. I'm trying to get used to it. I can't ever enjoy it because it's always about to end.

I said, "I think we're all right, we're all pretty happy."

She yawned, took her hair and tied it in a knot at her neck. "Now you're just being funny."

"No, I'm not."

"It's okay. It'll wear off soon anyway," she said.

Not so much wear off as explode in my face.

"One of us will crack," she said. "It's bound to be Frank, as usual."

"What do you mean by that?" I said.

I knew it was more likely to be me. Or the surface of the earth, to swallow me up. Or all of them, when they found out the truth.

"The Floyd thing," Edie said.

I remembered her face, wide and white. I remembered the quick tight shake of the head. "What about it?"

"It can't happen," she said.

"What?"

"Just don't talk about him," Edie said. "Don't mention his name."

"Why not?"

She looked at the ceiling, shrugged her shoulders.

"Frank won't like it," she said. "Just please don't."

I wondered what Frank had against Floyd. Maybe he didn't like the way he dressed.

"I'm meeting him later," I said.

"Floyd?"

I nodded.

"Why?" Edie said. "Why would you do that?"

I looked at her. "Why wouldn't I?"

"Of all people," she said, shutting her eyes, shaking her head. "You can't do that."

"Why not?"

"Where are you meeting him? He's not welcome here. He knows he shouldn't come."

"What's he done?"

"Oh God," she said. "Mum will lose it, seriously. Frank will go mad. That'll be *it*. Don't meet him, Cass. Don't bother."

Helen pushed the door open. I hadn't heard her coming. "Don't meet who?" she said.

Edie looked up. "No one."

Helen stared at me. I remembered her sudden coughing fit at the mention of Floyd's name.

"Is it Floyd?" she said. "Are you talking about Floyd?"

"No," Edie said, but Helen wasn't looking at her, she was looking at me.

She looked like someone who'd woken up too fast. She looked utterly lost. "Why?" she said, holding on to the door handle, turning it and turning it.

"Floyd's my friend. I want to see him."

"He's not your *friend*," Helen said. "What are you talking about?" And then she yelled down the stairs. "Frank!"

"What?"

She stood in the doorway, looking from me to Edie and back again, panic bubbling to the surface of her voice. "Frank, come here!"

"No, Mum, don't," Edie said. "It's okay. He won't go." She looked at me. "Will you."

Helen breathed in, ready to shout again.

"What?" Frank called from downstairs.

"He'll phone him, won't you, Cass?" Edie said to her. "He'll tell Floyd he can't make it."

"What is it?" Frank said again, loud.

"Please," Edie said to both of us. "Come on. It's fine. Don't bother him."

Nobody moved. I wondered why Edie was so keen not to let Frank know. I wondered why she was so anxious about it. I could feel her fear in the room, fear that quickened her voice and opened her pupils and brought a high color to her cheeks. What was she so afraid of?

Helen stared at me. I couldn't stare her down. I looked away.

"Cass, please phone him," Edie said. "Phone him now."

I didn't know his number. Of course I didn't. I said, "I haven't got my phone."

She said she'd look the number up.

"What do you want?" Frank yelled. I heard him start to come up.

Edie was almost beside herself. She was scared of him. It was like I was letting a monster climb the stairs. I couldn't watch it happen.

"Okay," I said quickly. "I'll phone him."

She breathed out hard, went to the door and called down to him. "It's nothing. Mum saw a big spider. We've got it."

Then she left the room and came back with the phone book, her finger on Floyd's number. She gave me her mobile phone. I did as I was told. I took it from her, listened to it ring. Helen stood just inside the room the whole time and watched me.

"Hello?"

"Floyd. It's Cass."

"Yeah. I'm leaving now."

"No. Don't. Maybe it's not a good idea."

"Ah."

"Sorry."

"I get it. I knew it."

"What?"

"It's fine. I'm sorry. It was nice knowing you."

"What?"

"See you around."

"No," I said. "I can't." I stressed the last word. I hoped he'd know what I meant. I couldn't talk in front of Edie and Helen. I couldn't say anything. But I still wanted to meet him.

"Cass?"

"Yes."

"Can you talk?"

Bingo. "No."

"Okay. So."

"So."

"So what do you want to do?"

I didn't say anything. I waited for him to work it out.

"I'll be at the clock tower anyway, how about that? I'll be there this afternoon. I'll wait."

"Okay. Thanks."

"Will you come?"

"Yes."

"If you can, right? See you there."

"Yes."

I ended the call, gave it back to Edie.

"Thanks," Edie said.

And I said to Helen, "Okay?"

Helen nodded. She wrapped her arms around herself.

I wondered if I was supposed to know what the hell was going on. I wondered if I was allowed to ask.

Helen broke the silence. It was like nothing had just happened, the way she spoke. Her voice was different, light and sunny, like she'd instantly forgotten.

"I'm going out with Frank," she said. "He's buying me lunch."

"Have a good time," I said.

Edie said, "Mum," and Helen turned.

"Don't tell him," Edie said. "It's sorted now. Cass has sorted it. Don't tell Frank. You know what he's like."

Helen nodded. She put her finger to her lips and smiled at us, and closed the door on her way out.

We were quiet for a minute. Edie played with the corner of a pillow. She opened a drawer and shut it again.

"Since when were you and Floyd friends?" she said.

"He's all right," I said. "I like him."

Edie shook her head and smiled at me, a wary, uncomfortable smile. "That's not what you used to say."

"What did I used to say?"

"That he was a weirdo. That he would never belong. That he made you uncomfortable. That he made your skin crawl."

Cassiel didn't like Floyd. And I'd wandered into another minefield. I had to tread carefully and back right out.

I shrugged it off. I said, "Maybe I'm trying to be more tolerant."

"Well, don't bother trying with him."

"Why not?"

"Test your new personality out on someone else," Edie said. "Floyd isn't our friend, Cass. He's not a friend of this family."

"What did he do?"

"He's a liar."

So am I. I'm the biggest liar you'll ever meet. Everything about me is a lie.

"What did he lie about?" I said.

"He said you were dead, Cass."

"So? Lots of people thought I was dead. You said *you* thought I was."

"He said he *knew* you were dead. He told everyone. He told the police. He went crazy."

"I didn't know about that," I said. "How could I know about that?"

"Well, I'm telling you now," she said. "Why were you suddenly so interested in hanging out with him? Where did that come from?"

"Why would he do that?" I said. "Why would he say that?"

"I have no idea," she said. "He said he had proof."

"What proof?"

"Exactly," she said. "You're not dead, so how the hell could Floyd prove it?"

I had this thought, and every cell in me stopped to look at it.

I wasn't dead. But . . . maybe Cassiel Roadnight was.

"It was horrible," Edie said. "It was sick and twisted. He wouldn't shut up."

I couldn't stop thinking it. It rang in my head like a bell.

"We were trying so hard to believe you were alive," she

said. "We were all just hoping. And Frank was doing *everything*. Frank—"

I turned away from the window. "What did Floyd say exactly?"

"He said you were dead," Edie told me. "He said he knew for sure, and—"

"And what?"

"It didn't come to anything, Cass. He didn't have proof. He was just trying to make trouble, and nothing happened. He's just a twisted, evil little—"

"What?" I said. "Just tell me. I'm going to find out anyway."

Edie looked at me. She bit her lip. "He said Frank did it."

It thrust me right back to the center of my own body. My eyesight was pin-sharp. My ears popped clear, like up until now I'd been listening to her through a wall. My blood stopped moving in my body. I swear it did. I felt for the cold, hard edge of the desk behind me. I felt for the chair so I could sit down in it without falling.

"Shit," I said. I felt the color drain out of my face. My thoughts careered into one another, out of control.

"I know," she said. "You can imagine how upset he was; we all were."

"God!" I said. My body was ice cold. It was warm in his room and I was shivering.

"Now you see why you can't meet Floyd," Edie said. "Why we hate him."

"I don't understand," I said, not really to her, just out loud.

"Me neither. It was a sick joke. And now you're back, proving him wrong just by being here."

"Yes," I said. "I am."

"You're alive," she said. "And he's a liar."

I didn't say anything to that.

"Everyone is going to see how sick it was," Edie said. "*No one* is going to talk to him now."

I concentrated on breathing. I thought if I didn't, I might just stop.

"How do I know why he'd do that, Cass?" Edie was saying. "Why would Floyd make up a lie like that about you? About Frank?"

I didn't know the answer to her question. I didn't know what to say.

Frank came up the stairs then, knocked on the door. I tried to see behind his handsome, warm face, his immaculate clothes, his smooth voice, his affectionate smile. Was there something darker in there?

"We're going," he said. "I thought I'd treat Mum. You'll be all right, won't you?"

I couldn't speak. My lips were stuck together. My tongue was numb.

"We'll be fine," Edie said. "It's nice of you, Frank. She needs it."

Frank smiled at me and closed the door again. I only blinked when he was gone. Could he be hiding something? I didn't think so.

If he was, he was better at it than me.

And if he was, did he see it written all over my face?

In an hour Floyd would be waiting for me at the clock tower. And I didn't care what Edie and Helen wanted me to do. I was going to go and find out.

SIXTEEN

never had a friend before Floyd. I kidded myself he was my first. It's sad, I know, it's pitiful. Because I kept telling myself from the beginning that it wasn't really me he was friends with. I knew it must be Cassiel. I just stole his friendship, along with everything else. I just lapped it up, underhanded and pathetically grateful, from the moment I met him.

I'd never known anyone my own age. Not really. Grandad and I tried making friends in the park a few times, but the mums were brittle and aloof, the kids were shrill and hung out in packs and laughed at my clothes. It didn't work out.

Grandad didn't send me to school because it wasn't worth the paperwork. That's what he said. He said it was a waste of his time and mine. I could read and write and count already. Apparently the rest was always going to be up to me. According to Grandad, school was nothing more than falling into line, sitting around waiting to be spoon-fed little pre-polished, government-approved morsels of information. Real life taught you to scavenge for your own facts, to track knowledge for days and hunt it down.

"I should know," he'd said. "I used to be a teacher."

So I got used to being apart, to spending most of my time alone. From the outside, a school playground sounds just like seagulls around a fishing boat, just like chickens over grain. From the outside, other children hide from you, shrink behind their eyes, until one of them is brave enough to get a stick and hit you with it, until another one chases you away.

Floyd didn't chase me away. That's why I liked him. But, then, why would he? I seemed to be the only person talking to him.

Floyd walked around in a circle of silence. Wherever he went, people stopped talking and just looked at him. They didn't bother to hide their contempt. If you wanted to clear a building in that town, put Floyd in it. If you wanted to silence a crowd, give them him to look at. I saw it that first day, when I went to meet him. I saw it straight away. He stood by the clock tower in his weird black clothes, in front of the little town hall, a one-man exclusion zone. I swear not even birds or vermin or insects dared break the rule. He was utterly alone.

I remember thinking we had that in common.

Grandad would have liked Floyd. He would have liked the way he looked and read and spoke and thought differently from everyone else. He would have liked the fact that he didn't belong. He would have liked all the things that set him apart, just like I did.

I borrowed Edie's bike without asking. I figured it was the least of my crimes. I asked an old farmer directions on the way down. He looked at the horizon the whole time we were talking. The clock tower, he said, was at the bottom of town.

"It's tall," he said, "with a clock. You can't miss it."

"How long will it take me?" I said.

He laughed at some fixed point in the distance. "Depends how fast you're going," he said.

It took me less than twenty minutes. Floyd saw me wheeling down the narrow passage toward him and he broke into a smile. I entered his airspace without blinking. I jumped off my bike.

"Hello," I said.

"I didn't think you were coming."

"Well, we need to talk," I said.

The smile disappeared from his face when I said that. He looked scared and ashamed and confused.

"So you know, then."

"Edie told me."

"What did she tell you?"

"That you said I was dead. That you said Frank killed me."

Floyd put his head in his hands and groaned. "So now you can hate me, like everybody else," he said. "That's fine, I get it. Are we done? Can I go?"

"Is that why everyone hates you?" I said. "Because of what you said?"

"I've always had a head start on least-popular," he said. "You know that."

"True," I said.

He said, "Try being half Indian in an isolated rural community. Try being an adopted half-Indian vegetarian who reads poetry and is called Floyd."

"And dresses like a circus," I said. "You forgot."

"Thanks for that," he said. "You were always the first to point that out."

"You're welcome," I said. "And for the record, I don't hate you."

Floyd looked up, taken aback. "You don't?"

I shrugged. "We're friends, aren't we?"

"I don't know," he said. "Are we?"

I said, "In fact, I was thinking of going vegetarian myself."

He looked baffled. He looked at me like I was playing a trick on him, like he was waiting for it to happen.

We walked to the river, to a place he called the warren. Floyd said he wasn't the best person for me to be seen with, given the circumstances. He said we were a pretty unlikely pair.

He said, "I'm surprised you met me anywhere public. People will see you with me, you know?"

"I don't care who I'm seen with," I said.

And he said, "Since when?"

We were walking through the town, headed for the river. People stared openmouthed at the sight of us. I don't suppose it was something they'd expected to see, the dead boy and the slanderer, out together. I was starting to realize they hadn't been seen much together before. Floyd kept his head down. He dropped his shoulders and his chin, and he moved through the open hostility like he was more than used to it. I pushed Edie's bike, tried to look friendly and avoid eye contact at the same time.

By the castle, a group of kids our age filled up the narrow pavement in front of us. They were shouting and whistling. Floyd shrank even further inside his clothes. I put my bike on the road and walked around them, back onto the pavement. I didn't really see them. I didn't really look.

"What did you just do?" Floyd said.

"When?"

"Why did you just do that?"

I looked at him. I didn't understand. "What?"

He looked behind him. They were suddenly silent and staring at us. One of them said, "Roadnight, what's with you?"

"Those are your friends," he said. "Those are all your friends right there. You just blanked them. You just walked right past. With me."

I had no idea. Of course I didn't. What was I supposed to do now?

"Oh. Hi," I said. I waved. They waved back, offended, speechless. A couple of them cursed me and walked away.

I didn't have time for it. I looked at Floyd. "Come on," I said.

"What?"

I carried on walking. I didn't want to get in front of Floyd because I didn't know where we were going. He'd stopped and was looking at me really strangely. He looked like he was adding up numbers in his head.

"What?" I said. "Come on, let's go."

He looked at me like I was insane, or he was worried for my health.

He caught up to me, got a little ahead, the way I wanted. "Whatever you say."

When we got to the church we went down along a footpath that ran beside the river. It was crawling with dogs. You had to watch where you were walking, for all the dog crap. The smell of it was sharp in the air. The footpath opened out on to a common, sheep grazing and kids skimming stones at a bend in the river. The rapids bared their teeth, a flecked white line across the width of the water. I wished I didn't have the bike. The air was wet. The ground was soft and damp and marshy. The bike was moving down into the earth instead of forward along it. Floyd walked fast, ahead of me. He turned and spread his arms, a black scarecrow in the middle of all that land. I followed, dragging the bike over grass clumps and sheep dung, cutting the corner carved out by the river.

There were four people on the common, three men and a woman, building something, the beginning of something. A sort of framework out of wood. It was taller than them already.

I pointed. "What's that?"

"Can't you see from there? The Wicker Man's beginning. It's that time of year, if you think about it."

We stood and watched them for a minute. They were using lengths of willow, winding it around itself, bending it into shape.

"Oh yes," I said. "So it is."

In two days it would be fireworks night, the Fifth of November. Two years since Cassiel's disappearance. Two years since my own.

Not a time of year I wanted to think about.

We cut off the path into a clump of trees. Floyd went ahead again because my back wheel got caught on a hawthorn. I had to wrench it free.

It was instantly different inside the little wood. It was colder and darker and dead quiet. I heard the sound of tread and wood-snap ahead of me. I followed it just fast enough to see Floyd's back disappearing into a sort of hollow. I left Edie's bike leaning up against the roots of an upended tree.

"Wait for me," I said, coming down into the dip behind him. "What are you, the White Rabbit?"

"Lewis Carroll or Hunter S. Thompson?" he said.

Like I said, Grandad would have liked Floyd.

We sat in this sort of dirt bowl of smooth, packed mud.

Floyd wanted Cassiel to start. I could tell he did. He just sat there looking at me, waiting for me to say something.

I said, "Why did you make up all that stuff?"

Floyd had picked up a stick and was starting to split it.

"What, that you were dead? All that stuff?"

"Yeah."

"I didn't make it up."

He smiled. He looked at me. How do you tell the person sitting in front of you that you didn't make up the fact that that person was dead? He corrected himself.

"I didn't *think* I was making it up," he said. "I believed it."

"Okay. Why did you believe it?"

He glared at me. "Because you made me," he said. "Because of what you said."

"Tell me about it," I said.

"We were both there," he said.

"I know."

"You're the one with all the answers," he said.

I dodged it. I'd sailed frighteningly close to the truth, and I just had to cross my fingers he wouldn't see it.

"Pretend I'm not Cassiel," I said. "Pretend I'm somebody else who knows nothing about all of this, and just tell me what happened."

149

He looked at me funny. "Why would I bother doing that?"

"Because I want to see things from your point of view."

"You're the first one who does," he said.

I made myself comfortable, shifting down so the small of my back was resting on the hollow's mud slope. "Well, if I'm the one who got you into this mess," I said.

"I guess you are."

"Go on," I said, "I'm listening. I won't say a word."

It happened at Hay on Fire. It happened right in the middle of the show. Floyd said, "Two years ago, two days from now."

He said the fire maze was alight, he called it the labyrinth, and the man with the fire whip was doing his thing when I came running up to him—Cassiel came running up to him.

He said, "You remember that, right? Him cracking his whip, making those massive great bursts of fire?"

"I remember," I said.

"It was brilliant, wasn't it? Utterly mad, but brilliant."

"Yes."

"How do you find out you're good at that?" he said.

"What?"

"Dipping a bullwhip in paraffin and making cracking great clouds of fire?"

I smiled at him. "I don't know."

"Exactly. Anyway. You ran over to me in the middle of it. You went right through the labyrinth like it wasn't even there, like you couldn't even see it."

"Oh yeah."

"Everyone was yelling at you, and I thought you were going to set your cloak on fire, your shoes."

"But I didn't."

"You must have been very high," he said. "Were you high?"

"I must have been," I said.

"Or very afraid. That's what I thought," he said. "That you were terrified."

He looked for a response when he said it. I didn't give him one.

He said that the band was playing, and the drumming was loud and low so it entered your body through your feet and hands and chest as well as your ears.

I liked the way he described it. I said, "I remember that."

"You were wearing a cloak," he said, "and you had a mask on, a black-and-red mask. You know the one."

I nodded. "Go on."

"I didn't know it was you, to start with," he said. "I didn't know who it was coming right for me in the dark."

"What did I say?"

Floyd looked up at nothing while he remembered it word for word.

"You said, 'I'm finished. He knows it's me. It's all over. I'm dead.'"

I didn't say anything.

"You said that Frank knew it was you. That's what you said."

"Did I say 'Frank'?" I asked him. "Or did I say 'He'?"

Doubt flickered across his face. I saw it there. "You said Frank. Did you? I think you did. That was who you were talking about. I knew that."

"Okay."

Floyd looked at the stick instead of at me. He picked at the bark, pulled it off in thin strips. "You threw your bag at me," he said, "from under your cloak. You told me to hide it or bury it. You said that if you didn't come back I should use it to get him."

"Get him?"

He nodded. "Get Frank," he said.

"What was in it?"

He dropped the stick. He scratched his head and shifted a bit and blew his hair out of his eyes. "Why are we doing this?" he said. "Why are you asking me that?"

"Just tell me."

He frowned at me. "You told me what was in it. It was all notes and numbers and stuff. Everything was there, you said, whatever that meant."

"What else did I say?"

A dog suddenly came into the clearing above us, stood on the bowl's lip, looking down. A Jack Russell, panting, his tongue lolling out of his mouth. I heard somebody calling. The dog licked its lips and ducked out. Floyd and I looked at it and then back at each other.

"You said you were sorry to land it on me, but I was the last person he'd think of."

"Really?"

"Yes, really. You said that's why you were giving it to me, because I was the last place he'd think to look."

"Okay."

"You said Frank knew you had it and that he'd be the reason if something bad happened to you."

"What else?"

"You said, 'He is going to have me killed. Frank is trying to kill me.' Is that enough?"

I swallowed. My mouth was dry. "I said that?"

"Definitely. Why are you making me do this? You know what you said."

"And then?"

"And then you ran. You ran off in the direction of the Wicker Man. And that was it. And I didn't see you again until this morning."

He smiled at me, a grave and humorless smile. No wonder he'd been so shocked to see Cassiel. No wonder he'd asked him face-to-face if he was dead.

I sat up a bit. It was hard to ask the right questions, to get what I needed to know and still sound like Cassiel. I knew I was inches from the sheer drop of giving myself away. Floyd was running out of patience. Why did I need to ask him all this stuff when I had been there, when it was me who'd said it?

"Did you see Frank?" I asked.

"Not that night, no. I didn't see anyone. I looked for you for a bit, but I couldn't find you. Then I went home. You kind of killed the night for me. You kind of did my head in."

Where did Cassiel go? What happened to him?

"Frank was there that night, though; people saw him. He was out the next morning, clearing up. And he was out with everyone else the next night," Floyd said. "I saw him then. He was searching, like the rest of us. He was kind of in charge."

"Sounds like Frank," I said.

Floyd nodded. "I kept out of his way."

I let my head drop back against the mud. I tried to put things in order. So Cassiel went to Floyd, afraid for his life, afraid of his brother. Why would Floyd make that up? What would he gain from it?

"What did you do with the bag?" I said.

"I hid it and I waited."

"And then?"

"And after a few days, when you didn't show up, I gave it to the police."

"God, did you?"

"Yes. I told them what you said."

"What happened?"

"They searched it. They said it didn't amount to anything."

"What about the stuff I left?"

"They said there was 'nothing of consequence' in there."

Floyd picked at his ragged cuffs, kicked his stick away on the ground. "They didn't believe me. Nobody believed me."

"Why did they say that?" I asked him.

Floyd messed up his hair with his hands, scratched his nose. "Why are you asking me that?" he said. "You're here. You're not dead. Frank didn't kill you. What are you up to, Cass?"

"I'm not up to anything," I said.

"Well, you're not making any sense."

"I've been gone for two years," I said. "I want to know what happened after I left, that's all."

"You lied," Floyd said. "You lied and you left. Typical Cass. And I believed you because I'm an idiot. It didn't matter because nobody ever liked me anyway. Good enough?"

"What did the police do with my bag?" I said. "Did they give it back to you?"

"No. Of course not."

Maybe if I got my hands on Cassiel's stuff, I could find an answer.

"Where is it?"

"Frank's got it."

"What? Why?"

155

"He went to the police station," Floyd said. "He was there for about two hours. I thought they must be questioning him, but then he just left with all your stuff. They questioned *me* for longer than that. I think I was more of a suspect than Frank was."

"Did you have any idea what I was talking about?" I said. "At Hay on Fire."

Floyd groaned. "Of course I didn't. Why would I? Do you?"

I wondered what Frank had to hide. I wondered if Cassiel had found out about it.

"I don't know," I said. "I don't know anything."

Floyd said, "Frank told them I invented the whole thing, and they believed him. He got rid of the bag, I'm sure. I would if I was him. The whole town thinks I'm some sicko who should be locked up, thanks to you and Frank."

I looked up at the trees, black against the pale sky, moving and grabbing at the breeze. "God, Floyd," I said. "I'm sorry."

"So, what then?" he said. "Come on. Frank didn't kill you, obviously. You're acting like you don't even remember saying all that to me that night, like you weren't even there."

I swallowed. I looked at him and away again.

"So tell me the truth," Floyd said. "I think I've earned it."

There was a crash then, the sound of my bike falling or something falling on my bike.

"What was that?" I said, almost glad of the distraction, and then Edie was standing above us.

Floyd got to his feet.

"Hey, Edie," I said.

She didn't answer. She just stared at Floyd like she was trying to make him burst into flames or disappear underground, like she wished with all her heart that he'd shrivel up and die. It must have hurt. It's hard, somebody like Edie hating you that way.

Floyd cleared his throat. "I should go."

I nodded. I didn't argue. "Okay."

Edie's sudden appearance had saved me. She'd bought me some time, and I was grateful for it. I nodded. "See you around," I said.

Is that it? his face said. *Is that all I get?*

I owed him. Cassiel owed him.

"I'll call you," I said.

"For Christ's sake, Cassiel!" Edie said.

"What?"

She looked at Floyd. "Come on," she said to me. "Now."

She went ahead, grabbed her bike and wrestled it through the branches like it was their fault, like the bike and the trees were to blame.

I turned to Floyd. "I will call you."

"No you won't," he said.

"I will. I promise."

"Yeah, right."

He was about to say something else. He looked like he'd just thought of it. I waited.

"How's Mr. Artemis?" he said.

"What?" I said.

"You didn't mention Mr. Artemis," Floyd said. "Doesn't matter. Just ask Frank how he's doing. Let me know what he says."

"I'm sorry," I said. "I've got to go."

He tipped his hat at me, and I left him there in a hollow of mud in the woods, cheated and friendless and still hopelessly in the dark.

"You're such a *liar!*" Edie snapped at me as we walked back across the common.

"I know," I said.

"I was so *stupid* to think you had changed," she said. "I can't believe I kidded myself that you'd grown up while you were gone, that you might even be a good person."

"What?"

"Stay away from that boy, do you get it?" she said, her lips white with anger, pulled back against her teeth. "Think of your family, just this *once*. Think of what we've been through."

But I couldn't think about them without thinking of Floyd as well, and of what he'd told me.

I believed him, that's the thing, even if nobody else did. I believed him because I knew something they didn't. I knew Cassiel wasn't back.

"I'm sorry," I said. "You're right. I won't see him again. I'm sorry."

I lied. Of course I did. I was starting to get good at it by now.

SEVENTEEN

I got good at lying when I was ten. Before I was ten, I don't think I told a lie. Not one. After that, I had no choice.

I was ten when Grandad had the accident. I didn't know that's what it was right then. I didn't know until later. At the time, all I knew was that he left at eleven in the morning to get more whiskey, and that he didn't come back. I didn't see him for four years.

It had been snowing. We'd had the coldest winter for twenty years or something. We looked out of the window that week at the sleeping, unspoiled icing on the park. We whispered so we didn't wake it. Grandad said he couldn't remember it ever being so thick and brilliant and spotless.

It was a great week. I spent most of it on an old enamel tea tray, bombing down Kite Hill. My arms and legs burned with the cold. My hands and feet nearly died. Grandad put them in a bucket of cold water when I got home, and I snatched them

160

out. I thought it was scalding. He said he watched me out of the window. He said I went the fastest. He said, "You beat everyone with their fancy sleds and their waterproof gear, hands down."

I couldn't get warm that week. I couldn't get warm and I couldn't stop smiling.

When the thaw came, everything was suddenly so dark and soiled and sludgy. Everything was ruined and dripping and black. The plants were black and withered from the cold. The ice was black.

That's what Grandad fell on. Black ice.

He fell and broke both hips. Just like that. One, two, three, snap.

He fell and broke everything. Everything got broken.

I was out with my tea tray in search of snow in higher places. I couldn't believe it was gone. I couldn't believe something so good could be there one day and gone the next.

I soon learned.

I should have gone with him. It wasn't at his usual whiskey shop. He didn't fall there. I asked them. When I got home that night at six o'clock and he wasn't there, I went straight around and asked. They didn't have his whiskey, that's what happened. They'd sold out and he went somewhere else to get it.

Funny, the distant little roots of big and life-changing things, their humble beginnings. The phone call that causes a car crash, the delayed train that kicks off an affair, the whiskey shortage that turned me into nobody.

"Where did he go?" I said. "Why isn't he back yet?"

They shook their heads and shrugged their shoulders and stuck their bottom lips out. "We don't know," they said. *Go away now. We don't care.*

It was the first night I spent on my own. It was the first of many.

I should have gone to all the hospitals. I should have phoned them. I might have found him that night. It might have been all right. But I didn't. I was ten. I was scared. I thought he'd left me. I didn't know what to do.

I was on my own in Grandad's house for over three weeks. Every day I thought he might change his mind and come home. But he didn't.

He lay in a hospital bed. I found this out later. Unconscious at first. In constant pain. Withdrawing from alcohol. Not allowed a drink. He must have suffered. He must have raged and ranted and seen things crawling up the walls, crawling all over him. He must have forgotten about me.

But when he was calmer, when he woke up and realized where he was and what had happened, he knew I was there at home, ten years old and penniless and waiting for him to come back. He was the only one who knew.

And he didn't tell anyone. Because I was his dark shadow. I was his terrible secret.

How could I forgive him for that?

And the whole time I was waiting, when people came

to the door, when the neighbors poked their noses into my business and asked questions, I lied.

I said, "He's just popped out to the shops."

I said, "He's having a nap just now."

I said, "It's school holidays."

"My teacher's not well."

"The school burned down."

I lied so much and so often that even when I tried to tell them the truth, they didn't believe me. Even when the police and social services arrived, and I said this was my Grandad's house and I lived there and they mustn't take me away because I needed to be here when he got back, they didn't believe me.

They didn't believe a word I said.

I didn't think about why Edie was so angry with me. I didn't think about it until later, when it was all I could think about.

She gave me the bike when we got to her car. She almost threw it at me. "You rode it down," she said. "You can ride it back up. It won't fit in my car."

"Okay," I said. "Fine."

"And go home," she said. "Don't you dare go anywhere else."

"Edie," I said. "I'm not a prisoner."

"No," she said. "You're a liar. That's what you are."

On the way back up the hill I tried to sort everything out

and make sense of it. I pushed myself up and along the lane and across the ridge of the fields. I breathed hard, in and out through my mouth, and the cold air bit at my throat. I kept my eyes on the mountains. They had been here through all of this, watching. They had seen everything. I wished that they would just tell me.

I believed Floyd. At least I thought I did. Floyd must be telling the truth because the truth hadn't done him any good. Why make up a lie that did that? And Floyd thought Cassiel had lied. He thought there was a joke somewhere, and he was the butt of it. He thought he'd been used. You could tell that.

I didn't know much about Cassiel Roadnight, but I was beginning to think I wouldn't have liked him. Had he lied to Floyd? What for? To cover his tracks. To fake his own death and lay the blame on his brother. Why would he do that? And what was he running from? Were the dark places in the Roadnight family so well hidden I hadn't seen even a glimpse of them? Was I that bad at looking?

I thought about Frank. If Cassiel was telling the truth, that made Frank a brilliant liar. A cold, calculating, flawless liar. But could he really be a murderer? Could he really kill his own brother? I couldn't believe I was asking myself these questions.

Who was lying? Frank or Floyd or Cassiel?

Was Cassiel alive or dead?

And if he was dead, was I living with his killer?

When I stole Cassiel's life, I thought it would be better

than mine. I thought he was happier and healthier and more wholesome than me. I thought he had a loving, stable family. I wanted what he had. Now I had no idea what that was. I had no idea who any of them were.

When I only knew for sure that I was lying, how could I trust anybody else?

Edie was home way ahead of me. The three of them were sitting close together at the kitchen table. It was dark in there, and somber. I thought I knew what they'd been talking about, what was so important that they forgot to put the lights on while the dark closed in around them.

I was uneasy. I felt sick with it.

"Hello," I said, breaking the silence. "Everything all right?"

Frank got up and put the lamp on. He didn't look at me, and I was glad. I wasn't ready.

I was pretty muddy from the woods. The ride home had made things worse. My clothes were a mess.

Helen's eyes took a moment to focus on me. "Look at the state of you!" she said.

Edie glanced up. She barely registered me; she barely cared.

"I won't get anything dirty," I said. "I'll go now and have a bath."

"Yes, you do that," Helen said.

It felt like they were trying to get rid of me so they could carry on talking. I couldn't be with them either. I was supposed to be home and I had nowhere to go.

"What are you going to wear?" Helen said.

"I don't have anything else," I said. "These are Frank's."

I'd stolen all this and I still didn't have my own clothes. I still had to wear somebody else's.

Frank smiled. "I thought I recognized them," he said. "I've got plenty more you can borrow."

Edie groaned. She smiled at something in front of her, and then briefly at me, a peace offering, maybe, but I didn't smile back.

"Let's go and find you something," Frank said. "Come up with me."

We took the stairs together. It occurred to me I hadn't been alone with Frank, not until now. I wondered if it was accidental, or if we had both avoided it. He put his arm around me, pulled me in. It didn't feel comforting anymore. It didn't make me feel welcome. I wished I didn't know what Floyd had told me, if it was going to turn every one of Frank's kindnesses into a threat.

"After you," he said at the top. He walked behind me to his room. I felt him watching me. I felt watched.

"When did you do that to your ears?" he said.

"Pierce them?" I said. "Oh, a while ago."

"They look—"

"Like pincushions. I know."

166

Frank went straight to his chest of drawers. I looked at the back of his head, smart and neatly cut, the collar of his shirt, his expensive cashmere sweater. I could see his face in the mirror in front of him, smooth and sleek and handsome.

I thought about Floyd, odd and scruffy and cast out. I thought about what he'd said.

"How's Mr. Artemis?" I said.

Frank stopped moving. His hands stopped, he held his breath. It lasted for less than a second, but I was watching, so I noticed. His face in the mirror was dead like stone, but his eyes screamed and burned inside that dead face, his eyes shone with horror and cruelty and fear.

He didn't answer my question. I watched his eyes flick shut like a camera shutter, and the torture in them was suddenly gone. They were nothing but blank. He turned slowly to me, his face composed. The drawer was still open.

He looked at me while time stretched out between us. He looked at me for a few seconds, but it could have been hours. I was aware of this pulse in the air, this febrile, beating tension, and even though he acted like it wasn't there, I knew he could feel it too.

"Help yourself to whatever you want," he said. "I'll leave you to it."

I wondered if he could see the damp, cold terror that crawled through me right then. I wondered if I looked as shocked and clammy as I felt.

Frank left the room with slow, measured steps. He couldn't get out of there fast enough.

I watched him go, and it was only after he left that I could move again. I went over to the drawer, grabbed some clothes without even seeing them.

What had just happened?

I wanted to go to Floyd. I wanted to tell him how Frank had reacted to what I'd said. I wanted to ask him what it meant.

But I couldn't go now because they'd want to know where I was going. And I didn't know where Floyd lived. I couldn't even call him because I didn't have a phone. I felt endangered. I felt at risk. Frank's reaction had totally thrown me.

I was alone and I was trapped.

I went across to the bathroom, locked myself in, and ran a bath. Steam blossomed in the room and quickly turned to water on the cold walls.

What was going on?

Who was Mr. Artemis, and why had the mention of his name changed Frank for that instant into something unrecognizable, something petrified and savage and in pain?

It was as if the smooth, confident, generous big brother I thought I'd met was just a mask, just a shell, and underneath something writhed, something dark and dangerous and afraid. And now that I'd seen it I could never forget it.

Was Mr. Artemis a real person or a hidden message, a code?

Why the hell did Floyd tell me to say it? I wanted to know

what he'd been trying to do, what kind of trouble he was getting me to cause. Me, who'd been so careful not to cause any. Me, who'd walked on eggshells and tightropes so I wouldn't get found out.

I sat on the edge of the bath, watching the taps spew out water, watching the tub slowly fill.

What had happened today with Floyd? Maybe I was wrong about him, and Edie was right. Had he lied about Cassiel and Frank? Why would he? For attention, maybe. Like those people who confess to crimes they didn't commit just to watch all the fuss start, just to be at the center of it. Nobody else trusted him. Why should I?

For a second I went cold all over. Maybe *I* was at the center of this. Maybe it was a trap I had fallen straight into. Floyd had sent a message to Frank through me. Mr. Artemis was a code that meant I wasn't him, I wasn't Cassiel. Floyd probably saw straight through me in the woods today. I wasn't nearly careful enough with him. Me and my stupid questions.

My heart thudded in my chest. They could all be in this together. Frank and Floyd, and even Helen and Edie. Maybe Edie had been rescuing Floyd today, not me.

Maybe none of them were what they seemed. Maybe it wasn't just me.

Frank had gone straight downstairs. Who would he call? What would he tell them? I pictured the police car cutting its way through the gray afternoon. I saw its lights flashing blue against the road, against the steep cut of the hillside. I waited for it to pull up outside, for the footsteps on the stairs, sudden and officious, the loud bang on the door. I steeled my wrists against the cold bite of cuffs. I steeled myself for the look on their faces.

It didn't come.

I turned the taps off. I didn't get into the bath, I didn't change out of my clothes, I didn't even switch the light on. I just sat there in the dark while the water lurked in the bathtub, turning cold, and all the light bled out of the sky.

What if they all knew I wasn't Cassiel? What if they all knew he was dead? Was I their alibi?

Somebody came upstairs, slow and careful and trying to be quiet. The light snapped on on the landing, cutting through the gaps around the door. I heard an engine start, heard a car back up and drive away.

The footsteps stopped outside the bathroom, a shadow breaking up the clean lines of light. Whoever it was didn't knock. They just stood there waiting.

I was sitting on the floor with my back against the bath. I pulled my feet toward me, put my chin on my knees.

"Cassiel?" Edie's voice said, slightly shrill in the cold and dark and quiet. "Are you all right in there?"

"I'm fine."

"What are you doing?"

"Nothing. Sitting. Thinking."

"Frank's just left," she said. "He got a call from work or something."

"Right."

"Something urgent in the world of finance," she said, and I could picture the sarcastic smile on her face. "He said he'd be back really late."

I didn't say anything. I sat there in my filthy clothes on the hard floor, staring at the shadows of her feet, wishing she would go away too.

Had Frank really gone? He might be waiting for me out there, standing right behind her. They might be looking each other in the eye right now; he might be watching her lie.

I didn't trust her. I didn't trust anyone. I was alone and I was trapped and I was as paranoid as hell.

"Are you going to be long?" she said.

"I don't know."

"Do you want something to eat?"

I didn't want anything from her, not from any of them. "No."

"Cass," she said, leaning her head against the door. I heard the soft sound of her hair, and her voice against it. "Cass, I'm sorry I got cross. You made me angry. I'm really sorry."

I didn't answer.

Edie took a step away from the door. "I'll leave you alone," she said. "Please come down."

I didn't. I sat on the floor in that cold dark room because

I didn't have anywhere else to go, because I didn't know what else to do. I sat there and I thought about the other times I'd felt like this. I thought about waking up every morning with pictures in my head, of rooms I've been in and people I've known and things you don't forget, even if you want to.

I sat there in Cassiel Roadnight's house, and I thought about all the other days and nights that jostled and argued and competed to be the worst ones of my sad and sorry life.

EIGHTEEN

When they took me away and I cried for him, they behaved as if Grandad didn't exist. They wouldn't answer my questions about him. They wouldn't tell me where he was. They acted like they didn't have a clue what I was on about.

I couldn't sleep on the end of his bed anymore, curled up like a cat by the fire on his soft velvet cushions, blanketed in the voice of the old man, lulled to sleep with words. I had to sleep in a stranger's house, in a series of strangers' houses. At the first one I wouldn't unpack my suitcase. If I did that, then I was agreeing I was okay with it. A lady brought me milk and biscuits on a tray. I didn't touch them. That night I ran away, back to Grandad's to see if he was home. They found me and brought me back. I didn't get milk and biscuits the second time. I ran away thirteen times, from five different places. In the end I had to sleep in a cold bare dormitory with cold hard sheets and cold hard faces, words as sharp as razors, in beds made out of metal bars like the bars of cages. I had to sleep there night after night, week after week. The months dragged on, and still I couldn't accept it. Four years, and there wasn't one moment of relief.

I couldn't sleep. I didn't. At first, picked on by the other boys for crying, terrified of everything that was happening, I lay every night exhausted and vigilant on my bunk. I lay at attention, listening for the next attack, planning, as a way to stay sane, what I would do when I got out, where I would run to the moment they realized their mistake and let me go.

Home, back to Grandad, and he'd be waiting, pale and familiar, smelling of whiskey, with a book in his hand and yesterday's wind in his hair. With a soft smile and a square of chocolate and a "Get on with you. Go out and play."

I kept Grandad to myself like a secret. I kept away from the others. I stayed hidden and I hoped, when they got bored enough to search, that they wouldn't find me. Sometimes they did, sometimes they didn't. Rigg and Fitch and Joseph and Connor and Bates and the rest of them, greasy, spitting, pus-speckled and choking on hate. They came and went, they changed faces and were always the same. They called me filthy names and made a game out of trying to hurt me. I told myself they could try as hard as they liked, it wouldn't work. They couldn't touch me because I wasn't really there.

After a while the adults tried to make me talk about

Grandad. They put me in a special room, like a treat, with pens and paper and carefully prepared expressions of sympathy and understanding. It made me more uncomfortable than the everyday brutality. They asked me gently and persistently if he hurt me, if he touched me, and where.

Grandad didn't hurt me. He never would.

I told them that, but they didn't believe me. They twisted reality every way they could to make it fit with their belief that they were right. They contorted it and bent it out of shape. Every week, at the same time, sometimes more than once, in that room with its bright colors and its forced, artificial comfort, they asked me questions and tried to make me talk. I dreaded it. It made me sick.

Sometimes I thought I would wake up. When it was really bad, I convinced myself it wasn't real, that my life was most likely a nightmare that was more convincing than the others, that was taking longer to end. That I'd be home soon.

I told myself it would be over soon for nearly two years. I told myself to wait, to be quiet and invisible and patient. I managed to fool myself for that long.

And when it didn't end, when I faced up to the fact that it wouldn't, when they told me over and over that I could never go home again, I fought back. I was twelve and I was bigger and I'd taken enough shit from them, and enough beatings from boys like Rigg, who thought that hitting hard enough made them important, made them somebody.

They blamed that on Grandad too. They thought I acted out and spat and kicked and threw and scratched and punched because of him. My frenzied bouts of anger were the scars of my ordeal, the symptoms of my trauma. They were Grandad's fault, not theirs. They held me down and waited for them to pass. It didn't cross their minds that I was violently angry because of them. They didn't think I acted out because I thought they were insane and in total control.

And then, four years after they took me away and locked me up, somewhere short of fifteen hundred sleepless, hate-filled days and nights, I escaped.

It wasn't like I thought. I didn't plan it. An opening appeared, a hole in my reality, an unlocked door, actually, that's all it was, and I took full advantage. I slipped through it and was gone.

They didn't find me. Not yet.

I knew I shouldn't go to Grandad's house. That's where they'd look for me—that was obvious. But I had nowhere else to go. And I wanted more than anything to see him.

Grandad wasn't there.

It wasn't his anymore. I couldn't go in. The chocolate curtains weren't just open, they were gone. The light pouring through the newly painted, impossibly clean bay window would've made Grandad cower and whimper and dissolve in his overcoat like a vampire; would've made him turn in his grave.

I wondered for the first time if that's where he was.

It started in my stomach, this feeling that he might be dead, like I'd swallowed stones.

I thought he must be. Otherwise he would have waited. Where would he have gone without me?

I'm used to that feeling now. I carry it all the time. He's dead and I know it. There's no way he could have gone on living like that.

But at the time, standing outside his house, it was just beginning. It was just a tiny hole, a pinprick.

I looked in at the white floorboards and Anglepoise lamps and showing-off flowers. I looked at the muddy art in gilt frames and wondered what they'd done with all his books. What happens to a dead old man's library? Does it go to a charity like Oxfam? Does it go to a good home? Does it end up in a Dumpster?

I asked myself these stupid questions so I didn't wail and tear my clothes and throw myself onto the road. I stayed quiet and still so I didn't get noticed and captured and locked up again, even though on the inside I was hollering and banshee-wild at the thought of my loss.

Grandad took me once to the back room of the Holloway Road Oxfam. I thought we were looking for clothes or something—I thought maybe he was going to buy me a suit like his—but all he showed me was a cardboard box full of glasses. Reading glasses, bifocals, lenses thick as bottle tops and thin as ice, big blue frames, little silver ones.

"Think of all the reading they've done," he said. "Think of all the things those glasses have seen."

It was like a box full of dead old people. We were standing in a room full of their clothes.

"What are we doing here, Grandad?" I said.

It was a history lesson. "It's what you *do*," he said. "It's what you *think* and *see*, not what you *have*."

"Is that why you brought me?" I said. "Is that it?"

I was eight, for God's sake. I just wanted to go and kick a ball around.

He nodded. "So you know nothing's worth keeping," he said. "So you remember this is where we all end up."

"In a rummage sale?"

"Exactly," Grandad said, with his hand on the hip flask in his pocket and his eyes still on the box of dead people's failing eyesight. "The Great Rummage Sale in the Sky."

I stood on the pavement in front of Grandad's house, and I searched the sky for some trace of him. I told myself that four years ago this place was his, this place was ours, and that somewhere those times must still exist, in its unused rooms, behind bricks and under floorboards, in its narrow attic spaces, between layers and layers of paint.

I stood there for less than a minute, and then I walked

away, because I had to, because somebody might be watching, because I wasn't ever going back.

Grandad would have been pleased to see that I'd followed his advice to the letter, not owning one thing, not weighed down by one possession except the clothes on my back.

I'd slept in the park for a few days. I'd washed in the restrooms in the playground, the same playground I'd watched through Grandad's window. I drank from a fountain that didn't reach my knees. I fed myself from the café trash cans. I stretched out warm in the sun in the day, and curled up wretched with cold at night.

I watched the house sometimes, from a safe distance, when I was sure no one could see me. I watched the lady that lived there. I watched her with her children, in and out, up and down, filling the place up, forcing light and life into its deadest corners. I liked her.

And then one day I saw her in the park. I was sitting on a bench, watching three crows attack an apple. I saw her coming. She stopped right in front of me. I looked at her and then I looked back at the crows. They were throwing the apple around, picking it up with their beaks and slamming it into the ground, as if they needed to kill it.

She sat down next to me. I moved down a little bit on the bench for her to sit.

"Hello," I said.

And she smiled and said, "Hello," back.

"I live across the road from you," I said.

She frowned and smiled. She looked at me and away from me at the same time.

"Oh," she said. "Right."

The sounds of the park carried on around us like nothing was happening. A man ran past with headphones on and bright, brand-new sneakers. A pigeon bobbed and twitched right by my feet. I jerked at it, and it flapped out of the way, half flying, half running.

"I like your house," I said.

"Oh, thanks." She smiled. "Me too."

"What happened to the old man that used to live there?" I said, like it didn't mean anything, like I was just passing the time of day.

"Mr. Hathaway?" she said, and I realized I'd never heard Grandad's name before; I'd never known it. She shook her head. She pressed her lips together until they were so thin they almost disappeared. She oozed silent disapproval. "He's in a home somewhere, on the Finchley Road. Redlands something. No, Redfields. Is it?"

"Where?" I said. My voice echoed in the empty cavern of my chest.

"Finchley Road," she said. "Definitely somewhere up there. Why?"

She looked straight at me when she said it. A kid fell over on the path in front of us and dropped his ice cream. He screamed like the world was about to end. She looked at the kid, and at his mother, who rushed to pick him up and soothe him.

I got up to go. I walked away and left her still sitting there, watching the kid, watching his ice cream, muck-flecked and melting into the ground.

I went to find him.

Greenfields. That's what it was called.

It was fireworks night, the Fifth of November. I remember sitting with Grandad in his squalid little room, watching the sky outside lit up and ripped open, hearing the squeals and whizzes and booms through the curtainless black of his windows, listening to my whole life fall apart.

I sneaked in. Nobody saw me. I didn't ask permission. I found his name on a board. Room 103.

Grandad looked fourteen years older, not four. I couldn't believe how much he had aged. He was frail and transparent and toothless. He lived in a room with a bed and a sink and no books. They had broken him. They had sent him to his very own version of hell.

I didn't understand what either of us had done to deserve this.

I stood at his door, waiting for his addled brain to recognize me. He stank of piss. He had cut himself shaving. The bottom half of his face looked like it had caved in. There was dried food on his mouth and his chin and his tie.

"Chap?" he said. "Is that you?"

I had to help him to his chair. He lost it at the sight of me, he turned to liquid.

"It's okay, Grandad," I said, lowering him as gently as I could, whispering into the white wisps of his hair while he wept. "I'm back. It's okay, I'm here."

"Where have you been?" he said. "Why did you leave me?"

"I didn't leave you," I said. "They took me."

"Who?"

"You didn't come back, and they took me."

I asked Grandad what happened. He looked confused.

"It's been a long time," he said.

"Four years," I told him. "It's been four years. I'm fourteen now."

"Fourteen?" he said.

"You went out for whiskey. What happened to you?"

He thought for a while, and then he told me about the black ice. He said, "Old bones don't mend very well." He couldn't walk properly, I could see that. He was in a lot of pain. I think he passed the time on morphine now, instead of whiskey. Part of him wasn't there.

He could never have looked after himself in that old house. I thought maybe that was why he'd had to move.

"Why didn't you come and get me?" I said. "Or send for me? I could've looked after you."

He shook his head. "I wasn't allowed," he said.

"Why not?"

The whole time I was away, the whole time I was locked up, it never occurred to me that he'd been under the same rules as me, that he'd been punished like I was. I suppose I still thought, until that moment, that Grandad was inviolate, above that. He was my grandad. Who would hurt him?

"Where's all your stuff?" I said. "Where are your books and things?"

He looked around like he hadn't noticed, like he was trying to remember what was missing.

"They came looking for you," he said. "They came here yesterday, or the day before."

"Who did?"

"They did. The social."

"What did they say to you?"

"Did you speak to anyone downstairs?" he asked me. "Did you see anyone? They're looking out for you."

I shook my head. I told him no.

"Be careful," he said. "They mustn't catch you in here."

"They won't."

"You can't be here," he said. "I'm not allowed . . ." and I could see that something in him had died. Some vital part of him was long dead.

"Not allowed to see me? But you didn't do anything!" I told him. "What did you do?"

Tears were pouring down Grandad's face. I wanted to kill them, whoever did this to him, whoever it was that ended him up like that.

"Why didn't you just tell them?" I said.

He didn't answer me.

"Why didn't you just say you were my grandad, and come and get me?"

Grandad looked at me then, and a little of the man I'd known peered out from his frightened, waterlogged eyes.

"Why did you leave me there?" I said. "What did I do?"

"Chap," he said. "I can't lie to you anymore."

"Lie about what?"

"I'm not your grandad," he said.

I thought I would choke. He might as well have put his cold, gnarled hands tight around my throat and squeezed.

If he wasn't my grandad, then who was he? And who was I?

"Don't say that," I told him. "Don't say that to me. That's what *they* said, and I didn't listen. I didn't listen to them, Grandad."

He shook his head at me. "You have to listen," Grandad said. "And I have to tell you. I owe you that much. It's the truth."

NINETEEN

'I've always been on my own," said Grandad. "I lived with my parents, in that house, all my life, and then when they died I carried on living there by myself."

I listened to him while the fireworks screamed and burst outside, and I watched him, this old man who was everything to me, who was all I'd ever had in the world and who was trying to tell me different.

"I never had a wife or children," he said. "I never had a friend, really. I had colleagues at work, conversations. One or two people used to nod and say hello to me in the library. I'd look forward to that." He smiled. "It used to be the highlight of my day."

He was shy, that's what he was trying to say. He was a certified, fully qualified, totally reluctant loner. Not just a bit awkward at a party. Crippled with shyness. Grandad didn't go out after work, not ever. He rushed home from school to see his mother, as if he were still a child, not a teacher. She was his best friend and the only person he could talk to. Their talks were fluent and easy. Perhaps she wanted him all to herself, so she never taught him how to be around people; she only taught him how to be around her. That's what Grandad thought after she left him. He was forty-six when she died, forty-six and friendless and a virgin, someone else's cruel and lonely joke.

School was hard without her waiting for him when he got home. Teaching was hard. His health unraveled. The children seemed increasingly bored and unruly, and even the other teachers laughed slyly at his hair and his waistcoats, at his awkward, stilted ways. He left before they asked him to leave.

His father, who didn't talk much, and who had always made it clear he'd never liked him, retreated to a room at the top of the house and hardly came down. And then one day even he was gone.

"Why are you telling me this?" I said. I remember my voice sounded raw and alarmingly vicious in that little room.

He didn't answer. I think once he'd started, he couldn't stop. He just kept on.

After his dad died, Grandad tried for a little while to be out in the world, but nobody noticed. How do you make your first-ever friend when you're fifty-three, and your own voice makes you nervous, and you're losing your hair, and everything you think and say and do belongs to another century, belongs to another time altogether? How do you stop and talk when nobody else is stopping, when everyone else has things to do and places to be? No one has the time to be pleasant to a strange old man who dresses like a funeral director and speaks like Charles Dickens. Everyone is far too busy for that.

He had money to live on and books to read. He discovered good whiskey. He locked himself away, too scared to do anything else, too old to start learning. He must have been the loneliest man in London. I picture him now, on his own desert island, right in the middle of a whole sea of people. He couldn't get off it because he just didn't know how.

"And then one night," he said, glancing at me, "after I'd been alone in my house for a very long time, somebody knocked on my door."

He was making sure I was still with him, still listening. Where else would I be? What else would I be doing? I couldn't move, apart from anything else. I didn't have anywhere to go.

"A young woman and a little lad," he said, kick-starting my dread. "A girl and a boy."

Their voices were loud in the empty quiet of his house. There hadn't been voices in there for years. Grandad couldn't cope with the sound of her, the boy's high wailing. He put his hands over his ears.

"I'm in trouble," she said, even louder. "I'm in deep shit. Let me in. Let us in, *please*."

The boy was soot-black and filthy. The girl's hair was

burned. He could smell it. He stood at the door, paralyzed by shyness and indecision.

She made his mind up for him. She pushed past him, dragging the little boy by the wrist, and they cowered in his hallway, cowered from the outside, from the rain and the sirens and the acrid fire smell that Grandad was only just beginning to notice, that he was only now aware of.

"I think I just burned a house down," she said, not to him, not to anyone, just into the air in the hall. He shut the door behind them.

"Don't tell," the girl said, starting to shiver. "Don't tell anyone, or I will come back and cut you while you're sleeping."

Grandad said the only thing he could think of, the thing he was supposed to, the thing he'd been practicing to a shut and guestless door for twenty years.

"Hello," he said. "Do come in, and make yourselves at home."

So they did.

He didn't have a TV. He didn't listen to the radio or buy a newspaper or join in in any way with what was going on outside his house. The girl complained about it. She said it was the most boring, half-dead dump she'd ever been in.

She was lucky. She would slap anyone who said it, and she'd have every right to, but it was true. Because if Grandad had known what was going on, if he had known that a girl and a two-year-old boy were missing, feared dead, in a fire in a council-run care home three streets away, things might have been very different.

The girl wasn't very good company. She set up camp in a room on the top floor, just like Grandad's father, and she wouldn't tell him her name.

"No questions," she said, "or I'm gone." And he didn't want her to go, so he didn't ask any.

She ate his food and drank his tea and smoked the cigarettes he bought for her. He assumed she was the boy's mother, because they had arrived together and because the boy wailed if he was ever far from her side. She was young, but she was old enough and she knew enough, she'd seen enough. Even Grandad could tell that, by the flint in her eyes, by the spark in them when she told the boy to leave her alone, to go and play in traffic, when she locked her door against his wheedling, and banished him downstairs.

"I remember the first time you came to my room," Grandad said, and I couldn't look at him. "You liked the fire and the clocks. You touched all the books on the shelf. You climbed up in an armchair and sat down and smiled."

The anger began at the edges, at the ends of my fingers and toes. I thought it was just the cold. I remember underneath all the hurt and confusion, this rational voice in my head saying, *It's cold in here. Stamp your feet. Rub your hands together. Listen.*

Grandad went on talking. He said I was plump and shining underneath the soot. He said I was resiliently cheerful and curious and self-contained. He said, "I think you knew more about life than I did when you were only two."

"Who was I?" I asked him, the cold spreading to my limbs, the rage spreading. "Who am I?"

"You're Chap," he said. "You were always just the little chap to me."

"What did *she* call me?" I said. "What did my mother call me?"

Grandad shook his head. "She called you Damiel," he said. "She called you a lot of things. But she wasn't your mother."

I was like Alice falling down the black hole, not knowing when it would end. I could feel myself falling.

The girl disappeared, apparently. She left with £100 of Grandad's money, found in a biscuit tin in the kitchen. She said she was going. She at least told him that. He found that he was disappointed—no, devastated, even. He realized that the few weeks and months they'd been messing up his house and taking advantage of him had been among the happiest in his life. She was on her way out the door when he realized it, her face set like concrete, her hair washed and combed and shining.

"What about the boy, the little chap?" he said. "Where's your son? Can't I say good-bye?"

"Keep him," the girl said. "He's not my son. He's nobody's son, as far as I can tell. That's why he attached himself to me."

I didn't cry when she was gone. Grandad gave me a bath and put me to bed and read me a book and sat up all night watching me sleep. I was as good as gold. I was the same the next night, he said, and the next, and all the ones after that.

"You were never any trouble," he said. "You brought me nothing but joy."

"You should have told someone," I said, the fury settling now on my chest.

"You slept like an angel," he said. "You woke up smiling. I made you hot milk, and you drank it and twirled your hair and smiled at me with your pink apple cheeks."

I couldn't look at him. I stared out the window at the littered black sky.

"I loved you," he said. "I taught you to read. I taught you to cook. I taught you how to be free and independent and confident, the opposite of me."

I didn't say anything. I didn't speak to him.

"Chap," he said. "I love you."

It erupted then, the anger, it poured itself out into the room like lava.

"Who's Chap?" I said, and the catch in my voice was bitter, caustic.

"You are."

"Or Damiel? Is that who I am?"

"Yes."

"Or nobody?"

"Not nobody."

"NOBODY!" I yelled. "NOBODY and NOTHING!"

"Chap," he said, "Don't—"

I don't remember what I said to Grandad, not exactly, not word for word. I was blind with it. I was thrown into this void, and there was only him to scream at, only him to hate. I let him have it, I know that much. I said he'd taken my life from me. I said he'd stolen everything.

"Where's my family?" I said. "Where have you hidden them? Who am I?"

I said I was nobody because of him, thanks to him, a lonely, bitter, selfish, *sick* old man.

"I hate you," I said, inches from his face, while he cowered in his chair, defenseless, remorseful, and defeated. I saw my spit land on his cheek. I saw the fear in his eyes, the fear that I would hit him, the half-hope that I might. I hated him with everything I had. I told him so. And then I walked out of his sad and filthy little cell and took the stairs three at a time and went out into the fireworks, into the night. I never saw Grandad again.

It was twenty-five past seven. I asked the man. I was nobody. That's when it began.

TWENTY

Frank came back in the middle of the night. I lay on my bed, on top of the covers, exhausted and fully awake. I heard him. He drove slowly into the yard with his lights off. He killed the engine and sat in his car. There was a long quiet space between the engine cutting and the sound of the car door opening and closing. He tried to shut it without making too much noise.

Was he being considerate, trying not to wake us? Or was he slipping in unnoticed, and coming back to get me?

He came inside with quiet care. The keys jangled slightly in the lock, the bolt scraped a little when he turned it. I heard the dog's tail hitting against something while it wagged. I heard Frank's voice, and I heard the dog groan with friendly disappointment. Frank took his shoes off and placed them neatly at the bottom of the stairs. I could picture him doing it.

I lay there rigid with fear, tuned to the slightest movement, the smallest noise. His feet whispered on the steps and along the hall and stopped outside my door. I'd wedged it shut with a chair. I'd barricaded myself in.

The water was still in the bath, stone cold and dead still. Frank's clothes were still on the floor. I hadn't left the bathroom until Edie and Helen gave up on me. I didn't leave it until I knew they were both asleep.

I think Frank and I both heard each other on either side of that door. I think each of us knew the other one was listening.

I'm not sure how long he stood there. Time stopped. I couldn't rely on time anymore. He sighed softly and went into his room, shut the door. I heard him barricade himself in too; I heard the definite click of the key in the lock.

I stayed awake all night. I wondered if he slept.

In the morning, before any of them were up, I took Edie's phone from the kitchen table and called Floyd.

It was pretty early. I knew I'd wake him.

"Who is this?" he said.

"It's Cassiel."

"No it isn't. No you aren't. Who is this?"

I thought he couldn't hear me properly. I went outside for a better signal.

"Why did you tell me to say that to Frank?" I said. "What did it mean?"

I could hear him moving, sitting up in bed. "How did he take it?" he said. "What did he do?"

"He didn't like it. It scared him. He changed. It scared me. What's going on, Floyd?"

"Meet me," he said. "Meet me down at the warren again."

I asked him if I could trust him.

"No," he said. "You can't. You can't trust anyone."

I looked at my reflection in the wet, clouded kitchen windows, blew the air out from my cheeks.

"Are you coming?" he said.

"I'll be there in an hour," I said. "I'm walking there now."

"Look over your shoulder," Floyd told me. "Keep an eye out for Frank on the way down."

"Why?"

"You're not safe anymore," he said. "That's why."

Floyd was waiting for me. There was nobody else but us. The Wicker Man had grown. His legs and belly were stretched out on the grass, like he was lying down, the two-thirds of him that existed.

"We'll stay out here," Floyd said, "in the open, so we can see who's coming."

"Are you serious?" I said, but I knew he was.

I flicked a stone into the river. It skipped six times and then bubbled under. The water was fast and angry and loud.

"What's going on, Floyd?" I said.

"You know," he said.

"Why did you tell me to say that to Frank? Why am I suddenly in danger?"

Floyd picked up a handful of stones and let them drop. "You might be," he said, "and you might not."

"What's all this about?" I asked him.

"You're not Cassiel," he said.

The last stone dropped from his hand with a *clap*. All I could hear was the water and the wind in the trees and the sound of Floyd, waiting.

"What?" I said.

"I know you're not Cassiel," he said, looking right at me. "And I know that Frank knows it too."

I didn't argue. I didn't bother. Floyd was utterly certain, I could tell that, and he was right. I dropped to a crouch at the river's edge, one hand on my head, one hand in the cold wet. I didn't say anything.

"You look so like him," he said. "It's extraordinary, really."

"What happens next?" I said.

His eyes and his voice were hard like set clay. "I want to know some things."

"Like what?"

"Like are you really not him?" he said. "Is it really not you?"

"It's not me," I said, and then I laughed at the sound of it.

"Then who are you?"

I told Floyd that it didn't matter. I told him I wasn't anyone. I felt that old familiar hollow where that knowledge should be. I felt the lack of my own family just as keenly as ever.

"It does matter," he said.

"Doesn't mean I can change it," I said. "I'm nobody. That's just a fact."

He didn't have an answer to that.

"Why would you do such a thing?" Floyd said. "Why would you pretend to be Cassiel?" I ignored the question. He asked it again. "Why would you do that?"

I waited a minute before I answered. I just enjoyed the gurgle of water on stones and the noise of birds and the open space. I enjoyed Floyd standing next to me, like we were just two friends out for a walk.

"It just happened," I said. "I didn't know how to stop it."

Floyd shook his head slowly, the look on his face half smiling, half stricken. "How does something like that just *happen*?" he said.

I didn't want to talk about it. I wanted to stay and I wanted to run at the same time.

"You are so like him," he said.

"Sorry."

"You're so like him, I can still almost believe you *are* him," he said.

"Well, I'm not," I said. "I'm not him. I just wished I was."

"Why?" Floyd said, and he could barely keep the disgust out of his voice. "Why would you want to be someone else? Why would you steal from someone like that?"

I thought about that moment in the hostel, stuck in a storeroom, looking at Cassiel Roadnight's face and seeing my own.

"Because he was handed to me on a plate," I said. "Because I am nobody and I have nobody. Because there was really nothing to lose."

Floyd said, "I look at you and I still see him, even though I know."

"Don't look at me, then," I said. "I'm sorry for what I did, but I can't help what I look like."

He didn't stop looking. I was like a really good forgery, I suppose, and Floyd was an expert, studying me for differences, for tiny things that were left out.

I asked him how he knew.

Floyd looked away then. He said, "I didn't know straight away. But when I did, it was obvious, really. You're very different."

"How?"

"Cassiel was never my friend, for a start," Floyd said. "I was a joke to him. The only time he ever asked me for anything was at Hay on Fire, the night he . . ."

"And that's how you knew?"

"You didn't know anything," he said. "You asked so many questions."

"True."

He shrugged and smiled. "And weirdly, you're nicer than he was. You're just different."

"You just said we were the same."

"If you're not looking, you are. I was really looking."

"Isn't everybody else?"

"People don't look," Floyd said. "They see. It's different."

"How?"

"People see what they expect to see, what they need to. Edie and Helen see what they need."

"And you?"

Floyd shrugged. "I suppose I'm one of the few who didn't need Cassiel to come back. So I could look at you."

"And Frank?"

"Frank knows you aren't his brother. Frank always knew."

I thought about Frank, how he had welcomed me in. I felt again his brotherly hug, his warmth and excitement and affection. Could they really have been pretense? Was he really that good a liar? That cold and controlled and heartless?

"How can you be so sure?" I said.

"Because Frank killed him," Floyd said. "Frank killed Cassiel."

"You said that," I told him. "And nobody believed you."

"But you do," Floyd said. "I think you do."

I asked him why, if Frank knew who I was (or who I wasn't), he hadn't said anything. Why hadn't he chased me from the house or given me to the police or hung me out to dry?

"Why was he so nice to me?" I said.

"You're not thinking," Floyd said.

I said I was too tired to think.

"Frank's never going to give you away," Floyd said.

"Why not?"

"He needs you, if you think about it. Frank needs you more than anyone else does."

If Floyd was right, and Frank had killed Cassiel, then I was his alibi. As long as I was there being his brother, I was proof that his brother was still alive.

It was obvious, if you were looking for it. And it was chilling. I had walked into a trap of my own making.

If Floyd was right, Cassiel was dead and I was living with his killer. If Cassiel was dead, then Frank and I both had a terrible secret, and we needed each other to keep it.

But how could Floyd be so sure?

"Tell me who you are," he said again.

"Nobody."

"How are you nobody? What does that mean?"

"I woke up one day and I was on my own, and nothing I knew was true," I said. "Not even my own name. That's what that means."

"What's your name?"

I shrugged. "I don't have one."

"What do people call you, apart from Cassiel Roadnight?"

"My grandad called me Chap," I said.

"Chap."

"Yep. But it's not my name. And he wasn't my grandad. We weren't related."

"Chap what?"

"Chap nothing."

"Where do you live, Chap Nothing?"

I looked at him. "Why do you want to know? Are you going to send me back there?"

"Where are your mum and dad?" he said.

"I don't have a mum and dad," I said. "I don't have anyone. I live wherever I want."

"Did you run away?" he said.

"Nobody's looking for me, if that's what you're getting at," I said. "Nobody's missing me. I didn't run away. I got lost. I don't exist."

"Yes, you do," Floyd said. "You're sitting right here. I can see you."

"Well, you're the only one who can."

I asked him why he was so sure Cassiel was dead. I asked him why he was so certain Frank had killed him, when even the police hadn't listened, when the whole town thought it was crazy.

"I wasn't sure until this morning," Floyd said. "I knew, but I wasn't sure until you called."

I asked him what had happened, what had changed.

"Mr. Artemis," Floyd said.

"Who is that?" I said. "Who's Mr. Artemis anyway? Is it a code? That's what I thought it was."

Frank shook his head. "It's not a code," he said. "It's the darkest part of Frank's dark secret."

"So tell me what it is. And how do you know it?"

Floyd laughed quietly to himself.

"What's so funny?" I said.

"Frank has got to be shitting himself right now."

"Tell me why, exactly."

"Only Cassiel knew the truth about Mr. Artemis. Only Cassiel and Frank. Nobody else in the world knew, and that's why Frank had to kill him."

"You know about him."

"Only because of what Cassiel gave me the night he vanished. Only because I worked it out."

"I don't get it."

"To Frank," Floyd said, "you're either Cassiel back from the dead, or you're his perfect watertight alibi, and you just sprang a huge leak. Either way, Frank is scared shitless. He's back to square one."

I thought about Frank's face, about the horror I'd seen on it, the glimpse of another person beneath, chaotic, lunatic, evil.

"What about Edie?" I said. "And Helen?"

Floyd shook his head. "They don't know anything," he said. "I'd bet my life on that."

"Or mine," I said, a little sharp. "Mine seems to be the one you're betting with."

A man and a dog opened the gate from the footpath to the warren. It creaked on its hinges and groaned shut. It wasn't that close, the sound was very small. We looked up and ducked at the same time.

"Is it Frank?" I said.

"Can't tell from here."

I thought about how empty this place was. How easily Frank could come and kill us both and walk away without a witness, without anyone seeing except the grass and the trees and the river. The grass and the trees and the river had never seemed more callous to me, had never seemed more useless.

All this time I'd been worried about Frank seeing through me, about Cassiel showing up. I needn't have. I was safe in Cassiel's place, the perfect piece in Frank's puzzle. I was home free and I didn't even know it.

And Mr. Artemis had ruined everything. Floyd had made me ruin it.

I wanted to be angry with him, but I couldn't. Wasn't what I had done so much worse?

"It's not Frank," he said, still looking. "It's not his dog, and I think that guy's got gray hair."

"Okay," I said. "Tell me about Mr. Artemis. Tell me how you can prove Frank is a killer, and then tell me what we are supposed to do about it."

He was quiet for a bit. We sat with our backs to the water, scanning the common.

Then Floyd said he wasn't stupid. He said maybe he looked it. He was willing to concede that. He said, "People see what they want to see, remember?"

"You don't look stupid," I said. "You look odd."

"Odd is stupid out here," he said. "It's a pretty straightforward place."

I didn't know why he was saying all that. I didn't see how it was relevant.

I asked Floyd why Frank hadn't come after him. I said, "How come he didn't get to you when you accused him? If he killed Cassiel just for knowing, how come you're not dead for going to the police? What makes you so safe?"

Floyd shrugged. "Frank destroyed the evidence," he said, still watching the man and his dog. "I'm sure the first thing he did was chuck all of Cassiel's stuff on the fire. He thinks there's nothing left to condemn him."

"True."

"And he thought I was too stupid to bother with, like everyone else does."

"Right," I said. "You're alive because you're stupid."

"That's my point," he said. "I'm not stupid. I made copies."

"Copies?"

He smiled at me, a small, shy, proud smile. "Of everything

Cassiel threw at me in his bag. Of everything I handed in to the police."

"Evidence."

"Exactly. It wasn't nothing, like the police said. It just took some working out."

"And what did it say?"

Floyd looked at me. "That Frank is in it up to his neck. And that you are not the first person he's killed."

Floyd said Frank was crooked. His flashy car, his expensive shoes, his handsome lifestyle, were all stolen, all incriminating, all built on quicksand.

"Everyone thinks he's this big success," I said.

"He is," Floyd said. "He looks that way, anyway."

"So who's Mr. Artemis, then?"

"Who *was* he," Floyd corrected me. "He's long dead."

"Okay. Who was he?"

"Mr. Artemis was one of Frank's clients, a wealthy old recluse with a fortune and no family. A perfect steal," Floyd said.

"What are you saying?" I asked him.

"Frank robbed him," Floyd said. "He stole his money and then I reckon he killed him."

"Are you serious?"

"Look him up. Lonely old millionaire, died of natural causes. Turned out to be a lot poorer than anyone thought he was."

"And you think Frank took his money?"

"I know he did."

"But you don't know he killed him."

"Well, I wouldn't put it past him. Would you?"

I thought about Frank's perfect front; his smart, successful, capable self. Could a murderer hide himself away that well? Could he walk around without a trace of remorse?

According to Floyd, Frank had a bank account in Switzerland, filled with siphoned-off money. He'd been stealing from Mr. Artemis for years.

"Well, how come he didn't get caught?" I said. "How come nobody knew?"

"Cassiel knew."

"How?" I said. "How do you find out about something like that?"

"I've no idea," Floyd said. "He's not here to ask."

Cassiel had left details in code, in a notebook. He had records of online transactions saved on disks. Floyd had spent hours going over them, weeks and months trying to make sense of them all.

"Everything's there," he said. "Frank's Swiss account, and Cassiel's account too."

"Cassiel's?"

"Cassiel was blackmailing Frank," Floyd said. "I worked out what he was doing. He'd set up an account of his own. Frank was putting money in there regularly. The amounts were getting bigger and bigger. It was all being taken away from him."

"So Frank had stolen from his client, and Cassiel was stealing from his brother?"

"Yes. Except Frank didn't know it was Cassiel. Not at first. I guess he just knew that if he got caught he'd go to prison for a very long time. He didn't know who'd found out about him. He didn't know who he was paying. But he paid because he was scared."

"He didn't know it was his own brother?"

"No. But he found out."

"How?"

"God knows," Floyd said. "Maybe Cassiel got lazy when he got rich. Maybe he spent too much money. He had the best clothes. He bragged about getting a car the moment he was old enough. He was flashy like Frank, flashy and unsubtle."

"You didn't like Cassiel very much, did you," I said.

Floyd laughed, but his face was grim. "I didn't like Cassiel and Cassiel didn't like me."

"So why did Cassiel give his bag to you?" I said. "Why did he trust you with it if he didn't even like you?"

"I don't know why he chose me. I think he was desperate. I think he chose the first person he saw, it's that simple. And he said I was the last person Frank would think of."

"So why are you doing this?" I asked him. "Why are you bothering?"

"Murder is murder," Floyd said.

"You think Frank killed Cassiel."

"I know he did."

"And you think he killed this Mr. Artemis as well?"

Floyd shrugged. "I don't have proof," he said. "I just think he did. Would he kill his own brother just for money? I think there was more to it than that."

"Okay."

"And if you've killed once, I think it's not so hard to kill again. If you've got everything to lose."

I nodded. "Murder is murder," I said. "And a lie is a lie."

"Nobody's died because of you," he said.

I thought about Grandad. I thought about Cassiel.

"But somebody's death could go unnoticed. That's it, isn't it?"

"Just because me and Cassiel weren't friends doesn't mean I want to see Frank get away with it."

"I understand," I said. "I get it."

Floyd told me again what Cassiel said to him that night, the night he disappeared.

"He said, 'I'm finished. He knows it's me. It's all over. I'm dead.' He was terrified. Frank killed him," Floyd said. "He killed him, and he deleted his own account, and he took Cassiel's."

"So Frank's account was Mr. Artemis?"

"No. Cassiel's was Mr. Artemis. You can imagine how that made Frank feel, paying back the money he'd taken from a dead man. Whether he killed him or not, it must have felt like revenge. Frank's account was under a different name."

Nothing was making sense. My head was swimming with it.

"And what happened to that account?" I asked.

"He emptied it. I think he emptied it and wiped it. I think he killed Cassiel and then he got into the Mr. Artemis account and deleted his own."

"Covering his tracks."

"Exactly. And then he wiped everything from Cassiel's computer."

"Frank said I did that. He told me Cassiel did that so nobody would find him. He said that's what the police told him."

"Of course he did," Floyd said. "He knew you didn't know. He knew you'd admit to anything he said Cassiel had done."

I blinked and swallowed, and it started to make sense.

"Cassiel's account was Artemis, not Frank's," Floyd said. "That's why when you said his name to Frank it would have floored him. You shouldn't know. That's why he's afraid of you, whoever you are. All the money went into Cassiel's Artemis account on the night he died. After he died. That's where Frank put it."

"Go over it again," I said. "Just once. Just simply. Tell me what you know."

Floyd took a deep breath. He held my gaze, and he spoke calmly, and he counted off a list of things on his fingers.

"I know Frank stole money from a rich old man who didn't live long enough to notice," he said. "I know Cassiel was blackmailing him. I know Cassiel set up an account in Mr. Artemis's name, and Frank paid money into it. I know that Frank found out it was Cassiel's, and I know that Cassiel tried to run. I know that Cassiel gave me the evidence, hard as it was to decipher. I know that Frank killed his brother and hid his body and transferred all the money."

"How do you know?"

"I've got the PIN," Floyd said. "I finally worked it out. A lucky guess, believe it or not—Zero-five-one-one. The Fifth of November. I've got access to Frank's Mr. Artemis account. There's more than a million pounds in it. I checked."

TWENTY-ONE

Floyd said it was up to me what happened next. He said as far as he could see there were four possible things that could happen.

"Number one. You could go to Frank," he said, "and tell him what I know, tell him what I told you."

"Why would I do that?"

Floyd looked at me. His eyes very dark, very matter of fact, unafraid. "There's a lot of money at stake here," he said. "You and Frank might decide to kill me, split the cash, and get on with your double lives."

"Don't be sick."

"You might want to carry on being Cassiel Roadnight," he said. "Don't you?"

I didn't answer him. "What's number two?" I said.

"Number two, you leave me out of it, but you and Frank agree to keep each other's secrets. That might work."

"What for?"

"I can't prove a thing because of you," Floyd said. "If you go on being Cassiel, then Cassiel was never murdered."

"I make Frank safe," I said.

"Exactly. Which is why he might not kill you. Which is why you might be safe too." Floyd tried to smile. "It's a mutually beneficial, symbiotic relationship," he said. "We did them in biology at school. Parasites."

"Nice."

"Well, I'm useless without you, and Frank needs you as much as you need him. You could help each other out."

"I guess we could," I said.

"You've got to hope Frank's thinking that too, right now— otherwise you're dead."

"And what about you?" I said. "You know I'm not him. Wouldn't you say something?"

Floyd laughed. "Me?" he said. "Are you joking? Who's going to believe me?"

He was right. I was safe for as long as I wanted to be. Safe, if you could call it that.

"Number three," he said. "You just take the money. Take the money and go and be Chap Nothing, somewhere else. You've got the PIN."

"So do you. How come you haven't taken it already?"

"I don't want Cassiel's blood money," Floyd said. "I'd rather have nothing."

"And the fourth?" I said.

"Oh, the fourth." Floyd grinned. "That's my favorite. The fourth is we get Frank."

He picked up a rock and smashed it down on the bank, splitting other smaller stones apart, showing the glittering wounds inside.

"How?" I said.

"I know how. But I don't think I can do it without you. You just have to decide."

The warren wasn't empty anymore. The man with the dog had gone, but a gang of eight or nine kids was coming, and a woman with her baby, and a couple holding hands.

"You should go," he said.

"Go where?"

"Go back to the house."

"And do what?"

"See how the land lies. Make up your mind."

I couldn't believe he was leaving it up to me to decide. Should I save myself and stay as Cassiel Roadnight, balanced precariously with Frank, but still balancing? Leave as a millionaire? Or should I throw it all away, and Frank with it?

Should I punish Cassiel's killer or use his death to my advantage?

Floyd had shown me everything, and now he was letting me choose. I think it was the most generous, reckless thing anyone had ever done for me. Anyone since Grandad.

"I've made up my mind," I said. "I've done that already."

"No," Floyd said. "You can't do it like that. You can't do it so fast."

"Yes I can."

"Please. Don't. Go home and think about it. Go home and call me tomorrow."

"Go home and risk another night with Frank?"

"Pretend you're on his side," Floyd said. "Pretend you're going for option number one."

"Where did it happen?" I said.

"What?"

"Cassiel. Where did Frank kill him?"

"Right here," Floyd said. "Somewhere here on this common, at Hay on Fire, when it was crowded with people."

"Is he buried here somewhere?"

Floyd nodded. "I think he is."

"How did Frank do that?"

"I've no idea," he said. "I wish I knew."

That's what I was thinking about when I got back to the house. I opened the door and walked into the kitchen, and they were all there, making breakfast, clearing away, and I couldn't see them almost, because all I could think of was where Cassiel was. How Frank had killed him. What he had done with his body.

Frank was perfectly, alarmingly, chillingly normal. He looked up from the table and smiled. He didn't blink. He didn't miss a beat. "Hey, little brother," he said with his mouth full, and he winked at me.

He winked.

I smiled back. "Hey."

Frank had already made up his mind about the choice I would make. Let him think that. Let him think.

Helen kissed me on the cheek and slipped her arm around my waist. She rested her head on my shoulder. Edie was busy at the sink. She didn't look up.

I would miss them. I found myself looking at the room like it might be the last time I'd see it. I found myself watching them like I knew I'd never see them again.

"You're still wearing those clothes," Helen said.

"I know."

"You look like you slept in them."

"I did."

"There's plenty of hot water," Edie said. "Have a bath, Cass, for our sake as well as yours."

I laughed. "Okay. I'm going, I'm going. Look," I said, walking into the corridor, opening the door to the stairs. "I'm gone."

"Good," she called after me, and Helen said, "Edie!"

Yes, that was it. Tomorrow or the next day, whenever it was done, I was gone for good.

I locked the door and ran the bath and got in it this time. I lay in the hot, still, stolen water, and I thought.

I was lying back with my head half underwater. I was listening to the loud drip of the tap, and the *swoosh* and *plip* of my moving body in the bath. Frank knocked on the door.

"Cassiel," he said. "Can I come in?"

"No," I said. No way.

He spoke quietly, close up, through the wood of the door. I remembered the first time I spoke to him on the phone, how his lips brushed against it, how loud he was in my ear. I wondered why I hadn't found it menacing then—his cool, calm self-assurance, his utter lack of surprise. I remembered him holding my face when he saw me, examining me because he knew I was a replica, because he knew I was a fake. I hadn't seen it. I'd been so vigilant and on my guard, and still I hadn't seen it.

People see what they want to see, that's what Floyd had told me. They see what they expect and want and need. I was no exception. Floyd was right. I'd seen a big brother. I'd seen what I wanted.

Frank's voice was smooth and low and predatory. He said, "I'm sorry about yesterday, about walking out."

"It's okay."

"I understand now," he said, "what you meant. I understand you perfectly. I think we understand each other."

"Yes, Frank," I said.

"Because we're the same, aren't we, you and me," he said. "And we need each other."

I put my head under again. I turned the hot tap on with my foot. I listened to the thunder of water landing on itself in the bath before I came up for air.

"Yes," I called to him. "You're right, Frank. We are exactly the same."

I lay there and thought about this sweet and ordinary and affectionate family, this perfect life I'd longed for, this slice of normal I'd taken without asking. I thought about my own family, wherever they might be, and if they remembered me at all, if they even knew I existed. I thought about Cassiel, who was murdered by his own brother and then robbed by me while he lay in his grave.

I knew what I would do from the moment Floyd sat with me at the river and laid out my choices, from the moment he told me the truth. It wasn't a question of deciding.

I was going to get Frank. I was going to find Cassiel Roadnight and bring him home. It didn't matter what happened to me. I was past caring about what I deserved. It was time to make amends.

You can't just steal a life. You can't be somebody else and get away with it. In the end, you have to give it all back.

• • •

It was a strange, gentle, tense afternoon. After lunch, Helen and Frank went shopping. Edie and I played cards. Nobody had any work to do. Nobody did anything. It was like a Sunday. I said so.

I said, "It's like the weekend every day here."

"How do you mean?"

"Nothing happens."

"We just sit about, you mean," she said. "Spending Frank's money."

The thought of it made me cold. If they knew about Frank's money. If they knew who'd died for it.

"I know," Edie said. "I think I might die of boredom."

"So, do something."

"Like what?"

"Get away," I said. "Get a job. Go to college."

"What can I do?" she said. "What am I any good at?"

"Lots of things. You can do whatever you want."

"What a load of crap," she said. "What have you been reading?"

"Okay," I said. "You can *try* to do whatever you want."

"Better."

"Go to art college," I said. "Do something cool. Don't be bored and spend Frank's money anymore. It's not worth it."

She looked at me funny. "Okay, Uncle Cass. I will. Thanks for the advice."

"Don't mention it."

She looked at her cards. "I've won," she said. "I'm out. I beat you."

I went to bed early. I was shattered from not sleeping the night before. I didn't know how I would sleep that night either, how it was even possible with Frank in a room across the hall. I knew he could come in and kill me at any given moment, at any time he liked. I had to hope Frank believed me. That I was just like him. That I was in it for the money. If he thought that, then I might survive the night.

I phoned Floyd. I stole Edie's phone and called him from my room. I told him I'd decided. I told him there was no decision to make.

"Move the money," I said.

Floyd's voice on the other end of the phone was hushed like mine, and just as urgent.

"What?"

"Hit him where it hurts," I told him. "Do it now, before he does, if it's not too late."

"I thought about that," he said. "I thought maybe he's moved it already."

"Have a look," I said. "If he has, then fine. He won't be around much longer to spend it. If he hasn't, open a new account and put the money in it. Rob him."

"What name shall I do it under?"

"Do it under yours. I don't care."

"I can't do that. It can't be a real name. It's a million pounds, for God's sake."

"Chap Hathaway," I said. "Call it that."

"Is that you?" he said. "So are you going to disappear with all the cash?"

"I don't want Frank's money," I said. "I don't want a penny of it."

"Okay."

"And it's not my name," I said. "I don't know what my name is, I told you. I don't have one."

"Chap Hathaway," Floyd said.

"No, hold on," I said. "I have a better idea. Put it in Cassiel's name."

"Why?"

"Because it's his. Because he died for it."

"And you're not going to . . . ?"

"I told you," I said. "I don't want it. I'm not him anymore. After this I'm not sticking around."

"It's good of you," Floyd said.

"What is?"

"You could have it all now, if you wanted," he said. "It's good of you to give it all away."

"It's not mine to give," I said.

"But still."

"It's the right thing to do," I said. "I couldn't live with myself if I did anything else."

We said good-bye. "How's it going to happen?" I said. "What are we going to do?"

"It's got to happen at Hay on Fire," he said. "It's got to happen exactly like before."

Hay on Fire. The Fifth of November.

"Don't sleep," he said. "Lock your door."

"Thanks," I said. "I'll try to stay alive."

I put Edie's phone back and stuck the chair under the door handle again. I lay in bed, too scared to sleep and too tired not to. Even when I slept, I dreamed I was lying awake in that room, listening out for Frank, waiting for my own death.

It was Helen that woke me up in the middle of the night, not Frank. She begged me in a whisper to let her in.

I opened the door to stop her talking, more than anything else. I opened it and got back into bed, because I wanted her to be quiet. She sat down next to me. We listened to the quiet in the house. We listened together to nothing. I wanted to put the chair back against the door. I wanted it all to be over.

"Is it because of what I told you?" she said.

"Is what?"

"Did you run away because of what I said?"

I didn't understand her. I wasn't Cassiel, so I didn't know.

"I need you to tell me if that was the reason," she said. She took my hand and pulled it to her lap and held it.

I didn't speak. I tried to see her face in the dark, but I didn't want her to see mine, so I kept the light off.

"I told you because I thought you should know," she said. "I didn't mean for it to hurt you."

"It didn't," I said.

"I know that's not true, Cassiel," she said. "He's a part of you and always will be. When you're a twin, that's how it works."

I didn't understand what she was saying. My brain felt thick and slow with fog.

"What? What did you say?"

I put the light on. Helen picked up my muddied shirt and folded it, without knowing, I think; just for something to do.

"You came into this world together," she said, while the quiet house seethed and whispered around us. "You and Damiel. I didn't want you to live your whole life not knowing about him. Was that wrong? Was I wrong to tell you? Or did I wait too long. Was that it?"

Damiel.

You couldn't forget a name like that. That was what the girl had called me. That's what Grandad said.

"Where is he?" I said, staring at her, trying to keep my

voice down. "No one told me. Nobody spoke about Damiel before."

Helen shook her head. "He's gone," she said. "And nobody knows. I told you that. It was a terrible time. Frank and Edie were in care when you were born, when they took you both from me. I never told them about him."

The room was spinning. I got out of bed and leaned on the windowsill and retched, but I couldn't throw up.

"Are you okay?" Helen said. "What's wrong?"

"Took us *both*?" I said.

I thought about the first time I saw Cassiel's picture, how it had felt like looking at a picture of me. I remember the wonder, the thought that out there somewhere was a person I'd never met, and had nothing to do with, who looked exactly like me. I thought it was a miracle, a parallel universe, a double life. It never crossed my mind that I might be looking at my twin.

"Cassiel, what's the matter?" she said. "I told you all of this. I told you this before."

"I must have forgotten," I said. My voice sounded odd. Helen thought I was being sarcastic.

"Don't," she said. "Don't do that."

"You think I left because you told me?" I said.

She nodded, searching my face for the answer she needed, finding nothing but nausea and shock and the closing of a terrible circle. "Or because I hadn't told you before."

"Tell me again," I said.

"Why?"

"Please," I said. "Don't ask. Start at the beginning. Just tell me again."

"Your father died," she said, looking ahead of her, not at me, looking into the dark room. "Your father died before you were born. Before we knew you were twins. He never knew."

"How did he die?" I said.

"You know that," she said. "Why are you doing this?"

"Pretend I don't," I said. "Keep going."

"It was an accident," she said. "At work."

"Oh."

"He fell and hit his head and—" She stopped talking. She gestured for me to come back and sit with her on the bed.

"I'm sorry he died," I said.

"I know you are." She took my hand in hers. "Your father died, and I had two small children and no family to speak of, and a baby on the way."

"Two babies," I corrected her.

"Yes. Two babies. And I wasn't coping. I let you all down. Those poor kids," she said, a crack in her voice, sniffing back tears.

"Go on," I said. "Please don't stop."

"Frank was nearly eight," she said, "and trying to run the family. It was hard on him. He bore the brunt of it. Edie was only two. I fell apart."

"What happened?" I said.

"I lost my children. For their own good. I lost my mind."

Frank and Edie were taken into care, that's what Helen told me, and then when the twins were born, Cassiel and Damiel, they were taken too.

"Just until I got myself together," she said. "Just so I could get back on my feet."

It took almost three years.

She said, "When I got you back you'd never met each other. You and Edie and Frank. Frank didn't like you being there. He thought you didn't belong. I couldn't tell him."

"Couldn't tell him what?"

She fought, and she won, and she got her children back. All except one.

"I couldn't tell him about Damiel," she said. "Your twin brother died in a fire when he was two years old."

There was this clamor in my head, this constant, blinding white noise. I looked at my hands on the bed. I couldn't see them right.

"I thought I'd never get you back when they told me," she said. "I thought I'd die from it. I didn't want to put Frank and Edie through that. They didn't even know him."

I couldn't see or breathe or swallow.

"You were there," she said. "They rescued you. But they never found him."

I couldn't say it. I didn't speak.

225

"They thought he burned up with the house," she said, rubbing my hand, as if to keep herself warm. "Damiel and another child, a teenager."

"A girl," I said.

"Yes, I told you, didn't I. A girl."

No you didn't, I wanted to tell her. *I just knew.*

"Did you ever feel it?" she asked me.

"What?" I said, but I knew what she was talking about.

The hunger that wouldn't be satisfied with food. The longing that wouldn't be softened by love or drugs or sleep. The unfillable space between me and the rest of the world.

"What?" I said, and then I said, "Yes. All the time."

And when I spoke, I sank down in the bed and rested my head on her. It was all I could do not to curl up in her lap and get her to rock me to sleep, all six foot one of me.

It was all I could do not to turn myself inside out with sorrow, with the too-lateness of it all. Because this was my mother. Not stolen, not borrowed, but mine.

I wasn't Chap. I wasn't nobody.

My name was Damiel.

But how could I ever tell her?

The twin I never knew I had, the twin I'd just found, the boy whose face I saw on a missing poster, whose face I recognized as my own, was dead, his body buried on the common, his killer alive in the next room. And I was pretending to be him.

Helen breathed softly and evenly next to me on the bed. She held my hand.

What would she do if I told her? Where would she break if she knew the truth about her sons? That one was dead, one was a killer, and one was a thief and a fake and a liar.

I tried to think straight. I tried to decide what to do next.

Tomorrow was Hay on Fire, and Frank was going to pay for what he did. I wanted to make sure of that.

And for Frank to pay, I'd have to tell the truth.

Helen would have to find out.

She'd lost a son, but it wasn't Damiel.

The fire didn't kill me.

Cassiel's twin brother was sitting right beside her. Cassiel's twin brother was me.

TWENTY-TWO

Every year, Hay on Fire starts in the town, outside the Parish Hall, waiting, holding its breath. The steam engine growls and threatens thunder at the head of the procession. The dancers and drummers and revelers stand behind in costume, unreal with silver and gold; swathed in black, hidden by masks; freakishly, skittishly tall; quiet, waiting. The children carry lanterns made of paper and willow. The stilt-walkers and faceless, cloaked sentries hold burning torches. The dancers wear red and orange and yellow, like fire, the band among them, their instruments glinting like jewels in the flames.

When the signal comes, the engine rolls, the drums start up, the band plays, the dancers move and sway and turn and rise and circle and do it again. The body of them, bedecked and horrific and splendid, squeezes through the narrow streets, gathers pace and other bodies, past the watching crowd. Stopping traffic, making its way with drumbeat heart to where the river snakes, where the land flattens out onto the common and disappears into the dark water, the line between the two seamless and invisible in the night.

I was there. I was in the procession. I saw it. I saw it all from start to finish. Helen didn't want me to go.

She said, "It worries me, Cass. It's like it's happening again. Like it's all about to happen."

"Nothing's going to happen," I lied. "I'm just going out to have a good time. We all are, right?"

I was wearing a black hooded cloak that closed over my other clothes completely. My face was half gold and half silver, my eyes hidden behind a red-and-black mask. Floyd had sorted out my costume. It was exactly the same as the one Cassiel had worn two years before. That's why Helen had objected. That's what she hadn't liked.

Frank hadn't liked it either. I was rubbing his nose in it. I was getting above my station.

I wondered if he knew yet I had taken all his money too.

I didn't think so. He would hurt me once he knew it.

Edie's face was painted a sickening pale. The shadows under her eyes were gray and blue and black. She had back-combed her hair until it fell, electrified, over her shoulders, almost to the small of her back. Her dress was white, her veil a soft gauze between her and what she saw. The red gash across her throat had dripped, staining the front of her bodice.

"Corpse bride," she said to Helen, grinning, before she

noticed me, before she saw what I was wearing, before she stepped back anxiously in time. I saw the fear come into her eyes. Her teeth looked dead and yellow against the white of her skin.

"Brilliant," I said, but she didn't answer.

Helen and Frank weren't dressed up. They'd go and watch, they said; see the procession and watch the show and the fireworks from the hill.

"And then we're coming home, aren't we, Mum," Frank said. "Getting an early night. Things have got to get back to normal in the morning. I've got to get back to work tomorrow, got to leave early."

His voice was strained, his speech brazen and well-rehearsed. The women looked at me with hollow, melancholy eyes. Edie bit her lip. Helen chewed her fingernails. Frank smiled, shameless and sordid and arrogant.

I knew, somewhere deep inside my mind, very calmly, that he was already planning to kill me that night. I knew I didn't need to say what Floyd and I had decided I would say, to make sure of it. I think he'd decided he couldn't trust me alive. I think he'd decided he couldn't risk it.

This is what it would be like living with him, I thought. Worrying every day that he'd had enough. Looking over my shoulder all the time, waiting to die.

I wasn't going to be a part of keeping his secret.

"Don't go, Cass," Helen said again.

"Leave him alone," Frank said. "It's just a bit of fun. He's not going to run off again, are you, Cass?" He didn't wait for me to answer. "He's not going anywhere."

"Hay on Fire," I said, my voice thin and airless, every cell in my body wiry and taut. "How can I miss it?"

"Be careful," Edie warned me, like she knew what I was doing.

The dancers dipped and writhed around me. The drums went through my feet and into my body and out my ears, just like Floyd said they would. He was somewhere close. He said he would be, although I hadn't seen him. I wasn't supposed to.

He'd said, "You do what you need to do, and don't worry about me. I'll be right there when it comes to it. If you know exactly what's going to happen, it won't work. Just do your bit and trust in me for the rest."

The procession moved through the town. We were on the uneven footpath that took us to the warren. The crowd funneled into the narrow space, the dancers faster, the drums louder, the costumes more striking and vivid than they'd been under streetlight, more real.

I waited for Frank to find me. I was expecting him.

I'd done what I had to. I'd done what Floyd told me I should. Frank and Helen had been watching outside the chemist. I saw them standing in the doorway, huddled against the other spectators in the cold. I ducked out of the procession for a second, black against the dark, unnoticed, really. I smiled at Helen, my mother, kissed her on the cheek, and I leaned in to Frank, spoke simply and clearly into his ear.

"The deal is off," I said. "You're not safe. I have Mr. Artemis. I've changed his name. I've taken your money and tomorrow I'm going to tell. To stop me, you'll have to kill me like you killed your other brother."

Frank didn't notice the "other." He kept his face still, kept the smile on it that he had arranged there. There was nothing he could do, not with Helen next to him. His eyes burned, dark and furious and livid, the monster inside the man. I felt the heat of his breath on my neck. Three words. Calmly and surely spoken.

"So you're dead."

I joined the procession again, slipped back in and flowed on. I wondered how he would do it. In a crowd like this, now, here, in the dark, something fast like a knife, something quiet like that, quick and easy, if you knew what you were doing.

Or something slower, just me and him in the dark somewhere, with the sound of the crowd behind us, with no one there to see.

I wondered if he planned to kill me the same way he killed Cassiel. And I thought that maybe I deserved it, to die the same way as the brother whose life I had stolen.

Please, God, let Floyd be somewhere, I thought. Please, God, make sure he gets this down.

The crowd settled on the slope of the common, and the procession wound its way ahead of them down to the flat land, to where the willow creatures and the circular labyrinths and the giant Wicker Man all awaited their fate, their beautiful burning.

I stood to one side, quiet and watchful and, I hoped, unseen in the center of the show, in the middle of the chaos and activity. The music boomed. The flames cracked and flickered. The performers waited on the edge of the circle, practicing, their fire toys cutting the air with loud, rhythmic sighs. The smell of paraffin was thick and acrid in the air. Wires ran across the field, this way and that, a network of connections. The chimneys belched flame like breath, like sleeping dragons. The fireworks bided silently in the ground, their noise and energy and light shut in, poised. It was curiously quiet where I stood, in the eye of the storm. I saw everything and nothing at the same time. It was deafening and without sound, all at once. I wondered if these were the last things I would see, the last sounds I'd hear. I was surprised to find how sad I was, if this was it, if I was going.

I didn't want to die. It seemed so unfair. I'd just found out who I was.

I saw Frank first, now in red and black, disguised, coming toward me across the burning floor, the everyday mask gone from his face, the black mask he wore hiding none of his rage.

A willow man and child held hands behind him, their outlines bright with flame against the black sky. The gasp of the crowd retreated suddenly. I lost it. There was only Frank.

I knew what he'd done. He'd gone home. He'd taken Helen to bed. He'd given her an extra pill so she would sleep without waking. He'd made a big show of going to bed too. She was his alibi. I knew how Frank worked. Weren't we the same? Now he was coming at me, cold and purposeful, with nothing but murder in his eyes.

Shit! I thought. I might even have said it out loud. "Floyd, where are you?"

And then I saw Floyd too, coming from the other direction, headed straight for us. I don't know how I could tell it was him. Wild and stunning and resplendent, the circus boy risen above shame, the phoenix from the ashes. Frank would never recognize him. He could be inches from us, and Frank wouldn't know it. Nobody would.

Floyd was taller than I'd thought possible, his stilted legs draped in cloth, his blackened face almost invisible beneath a huge and flaming dragon, its wings guided by steel rods in his hands, its spine a mass of writhing flags and banners, its head strangely mobile, graceful and fluent.

He took my breath away.

And then Frank did. He grabbed me by the throat and he carried me, despite my struggling weight, despite my kicking and grabbing and throttled screaming, down to the edge of the river, down into a dip where the light from the fires didn't reach, where the sound didn't travel. The water glowed strange and green under the sky. It slipped past, oblivious.

"You're dead," Frank said, and he threw me hard onto the ground. The stones bit into my back and my shoulder and my legs.

"How are you going to kill me, Frank?" I said, the hurt and rage in my voice sounding like bravado. "The same way you killed Cassiel?"

I felt something in the bushes just to my left. I didn't see it or hear it, I just felt it, like an intake of breath. Was that Floyd?

He was right here. Was he recording this? Was my death going according to plan?

"Where's my money?" Frank said. "Where have you put it?"

"I've given it to Cassiel," I said. "I've put it in his name. He earned it, don't you think?"

Frank hit me hard across the face with the back of his hand. It went numb for a second, I felt nothing, and then the pain rushed in to fill the sudden vacuum—my cheek burning, my jaw alight. I reeled, tried to get up from where I was, down in the mud and the stones.

"So you're stealing it," he said. "You've taken his place and now you're taking my money."

"I don't want a penny," I said. "I don't want any part of what you killed Cassiel for."

He hit me again.

"Shall I feed you to the Wicker Man too?" he said. "Knock you out with Helen's drugs and stuff you in his belly while the flames are licking at his legs? I think you're too big for that now, whoever you are. I think you've outgrown it."

"Is that what you did to him?" I said, scuttling away from his hands.

"I think I'll drown you," he said. "I think you'll fall and hit your head and breathe in river water. Such a shame, with you just back. Such a tragedy."

"Where is he?" I said. "Where did you put my brother?"

"*Your* brother?" Frank said, and he hit me again, harder this time, across the side of my head. At the same time, the first firework went off above us, a screaming, terrified bolt of white light that burst open, drawing sighs from the mouth of the crowd, illuminating the look of pure hatred on his face. "Who are you?" he said, grabbing me by my hair, pulling me to my feet.

My jaw ached, my head spun. There was a stabbing pain in my cheek, like a pulse. The bush rustled, I heard it. I saw someone in it move.

"I am Damiel Roadnight." I said it out loud for the first time. I felt sad and proud to say it. "Your brother. I'm Cassiel's twin. You didn't know about me, did you?"

The crowd sighed again to red and green rockets, to a burst of silver that fell slowly, like water glinting in sunlight.

"You and I are not the same, Frank," I told him while he readied himself to hit me. "But Cassiel and I were. We were identical. I came back to avenge him."

And I hit Frank on the side of the head as hard as I could, with a rock I'd picked up from the ground. I hit him again as he was going down, and he lost consciousness and fell, crumpled and loose at my feet.

At the same time, I saw Floyd's dragon rushing toward us from where the fireworks shot up, from where the flames were leaping up the Wicker Man's frame, hot and suddenly loud and crackling, turning the dark sky light, turning night into nothing like day. He wasn't close enough. He hadn't got it. It was all for nothing. What had I imagined in the bushes? What had I seen and heard?

A white figure, small and hunched and trembling, with black, back-combed hair and gray shadows under her eyes. Edie stood up. She had heard everything. She held her phone out in her shaking hand for Floyd and me to see. Floyd hadn't got it like we planned, but Edie had recorded it all.

TWENTY-THREE

Cassiel's body had burned up to almost nothing in the Wicker Man. Nobody had seen Frank pack the Wicker Man with extra wood and wool and fiber, with chemical-soaked towels to explode and boost the temperature to make it hot enough to rob a body of its flesh before the fire died. Nobody'd seen him climb up the ladder, Cassiel slung over his shoulder, drugged and wrapped in sackcloth. It was a good Wicker Man that year, that's what everybody said. It was especially dramatic.

Frank had stayed behind afterward to help clear up. He'd done it before. It wasn't anything special. The hole was already dug for all the hot ashes. Frank scooped what was left of the Wicker Man and his brother inside it. My brother. Mine and Frank's and Edie's.

No one noticed Cassiel was missing until the morning. By the time Helen raised the alarm and Frank led the search, all concern and brotherly love, Cassiel was tidied away, his computer was wiped. All trace of him was gone.

Except what he had given to Floyd.

And nobody believed Floyd. Not the first time.

He called the police on Edie's phone. I stood over Frank with a rock in my hand just in case he woke up before they got there. I wasn't afraid to hit him again. I wasn't shy of doing it. I wanted to.

Edie shook. Her eyes were glassy.

"Why are you here?" I said.

She looked straight through me. She didn't answer.

Floyd took his costume off and laid it on the ground. It flapped feebly in the wind, a defeated dragon.

"Why is Edie here?" I said. "Why did you drag her into this?"

"I didn't," Floyd said.

"What?"

"Believe it or not, *she* came to *me*."

He didn't have time to explain. A police car crossing the common and stopping by the river wasn't so unusual, not on a night like this. The police were everywhere. We gave them Edie's phone. They wrapped a blanket around her shoulders. She told them what she had seen and heard, what she had recorded. They picked Frank up like a dead weight and put him in the car. He groaned a little, and the sound of him waking up made me realize how afraid I'd been, made me see how close

I'd come to dying, how close Cassiel had come to dying twice.

Floyd drove us home in Edie's car. She still couldn't stop shaking.

"Helen's asleep," I said. "Frank gave her extra medicine." And as soon as I said it, Edie's panic broke, like the quick white crashing of a wave. It spilled out all over the car, stealing the oxygen.

Her voice was rushed and broken. "I can't do this," she said.

She opened her door and tried to get out while the car was still moving. She was outside in the dark as soon as we stopped, all in white and white-faced, like a ghost. Floyd got out. I stayed where I was. I thought if I tried to go near her, she might run away. I watched through my window. Her hands were fists at her side, her mouth a black hole, the muscles in her neck straining.

"I can't do this," she shouted. "Oh God!"

I didn't know what to do. I bent down and put my head in my hands. She was my sister, and she wasn't my sister anymore. I had everything and nothing at the same time.

"Edie," said Floyd, his voice low and steady. It moved toward her in the dark just like he did.

She turned away from him, stepped farther from the car. She almost disappeared into the darkness. She held on to herself and rocked.

"Who is he?" she moaned.

Floyd looked at me through the window. "He's your brother."

When I'd told him that night that I was Cassiel's twin, Floyd had smiled quickly and bent double and covered his eyes. Then he'd hugged me. He said he was happy and sorry at the same time. He said "Why?" and "How?" and we knew we had plenty of time to talk about everything, later.

I waited. I waited for what Edie would say.

"What's our grandmother's name?" she said to me through the glass. She was shouting.

"What?"

"What was our first dog called? What's my favorite color? When's Mum's birthday?"

"I don't know," I said.

"What film do we always watch at Christmas?"

"Edie—"

"Shut up!" she said. "Get out of my car."

I got out and faced her across the grimy wet-stained silver of the roof. Floyd looked at me. The black hadn't come off his face. It was smeared and half wiped. His face was disappearing into the dark, like he was vanishing.

"Who are you?" she said.

"Why did you help me, Edie?" I asked.

She looked at the black sky and at Floyd. She wouldn't look at me.

"Why were you there?" I said.

"I thought he was going to kill you," she said.

"Who? Frank?"

She nodded.

"So did I," I said.

"Why did you think that?" I asked. "What happened?"

She still wouldn't look at me. She said, "The night you hid in the bathroom and wouldn't come out. The night he went off and came back in the middle of the night."

"What about it?"

"He was raging," she said. "He was mad with it, like he used to be. I hadn't seen him like that in ages. You were scared. I knew you were. I knew something was wrong."

I breathed out.

"So you went to Floyd?"

Edie nodded. "Only this morning. I just wanted to ask him something."

She looked at me then for the first time. Looked at me, not at Cassiel. I could feel the difference, like a gap in the air.

"You're not him," Edie said quietly, and every single fear in me reared up and howled when she said it.

I didn't say anything.

"You're not Cassiel," she said.

It was so simple, so clear and definite.

"No," I said, "I'm not him."

"Cassiel's dead," she said.

"Yes."

"And who are you?"

"I'm his brother. And I'm yours. I didn't know it until yesterday."

"Who told you?" she said. "Who told you that?"

"Helen," I said. "She told me. She told Cassiel."

We didn't stop looking at each other. Neither of us looked away. Edie's eyes went hollow. I watched it happen. I watched her remove herself from me, retreat down a corridor of locked doors. She wasn't looking at her brother anymore.

She opened her mouth to scream, to curse me, to remind me of my place in the world.

I didn't wait to hear it. You don't stand there and take it when someone damns you for all eternity, even if you deserve it. You try and dodge their words, though you know they're coming straight for you, like a bullet, like a smart missile.

You run.

TWENTY-FOUR

I t was Floyd that came and found me. I hoped he would. I
didn't have the strength to run anymore. I went back to the
warren, picked through the dying crowd and the sea of litter,
to the little wood, and I curled up in the mud bowl he'd taken
me to. I curled up in the cold, and at some point I slept.

He woke me up gently, with a hand on my shoulder. His
face and clothes were clean, but he still looked as if he'd just
come from the circus. He still looked like a clown.

"Chap," he said. "Damiel. Wake up. Time to go home."

He took me up to the house. He took me up on the back
of his bike. It was hard going, up the hills. I got off and walked
most of the way.

"She wanted to help," he said. "When I told her, Edie
wanted to help. Remember that."

On the way up I thought about Grandad. I thought about
what I would say if he was still alive. I thought about saying

sorry. I wanted to tell him I still loved him, even if he couldn't hear. I wished I could make my peace with him, just like I wanted Edie and Helen to make theirs with me, their impostor, their fake, their thief and liar, their brother and son.

We all take things that don't belong to us, I thought, and I told Grandad, wherever he was, even though I knew he couldn't hear. We all want what we haven't got.

Frank's car was in the yard. It was the first thing I saw. The sight of it stopped me dead.

Floyd put his hand on my arm, just like he did that first day on the hill to see if I was living or a ghost, when I was both.

"It's okay," he said. "He isn't here."

There was a police car too. There were police in the kitchen when Floyd and I walked in. Edie was still in her costume. She'd been crying, and her eyes were as red as the faded fake blood on her dress. She looked at me and didn't look away.

"Hi," I said.

Helen was sitting at the table, smoking a cigarette. A policewoman was holding her hand.

She stood up. Helen stood up. Her nails were bitten to the quick, and her bangles rang just like the first time I saw her, just like when Cassiel came home. She was shaking, but she stood up and walked toward me.

"Damiel?" she said, in the smallest, softest voice—a smile

almost on her lips, her eyes sadder and angrier than I could bear, the tears in her eyes pulling at the tears in mine. My mother.

"Damiel?" she said, and Edie was crying again too. "Is that you?"

"Yes, Mum," I said. "Yes. I think it's me."